Praise for Deepti Kapoor's

A BAD CHARACTER

"Captivating. . . . *A Bad Character* echoes Nabokov's *Lolita* with a story about the sexual initiation of a young woman, but offers a female perspective, one that doesn't pull any punches. . . . Literary voices like Kapoor's . . . are now more crucial than ever."   —*The Rumpus*

"Spellbinding: Here is a novel about sex, about drugs, about a city on the brink of awe-inspiring and terrible change."   —Nell Freudenberger,
author of *The Newlyweds*

"India, once again. Its dark underbelly—flashing images of poverty and squalor, corruption and drugs and, above all, battered lives. . . . Here's a young woman, named Deepti Kapoor, picking up where the others have left off, adding something here (a female protagonist), subtracting something there (sentiment), splashing into our lives like the beginning of the monsoon hitting Delhi's streets. And the irony of it all? By the last page you have to ask yourself who is the bad character of her title: the unnamed female narrator . . . or the man whose life she believes she has unpacked so carefully."   —*CounterPunch*

"A stylishly written, powerfully moving love story. . . . What *Twilight in Delhi* is to the twentieth-century Indian novel, *A Bad Character* is to the twenty-first: the essence of India's corrupt capital, brilliantly and darkly distilled. This is a remarkable debut from a major new talent."
—William Dalrymple, author of *The Last Mughal*

"Riveting. . . . Kapoor's debut novel is a coming-of-age tale as complex and gritty and frankly terrifying as Delhi, the city that forms its backdrop." —*Bustle*

"An intimate, raw exploration of [a] profound transformation." —*Booklist*

"Sharply told." —*Largehearted Boy*

"Haunting. . . . A beguiling, hallucinatory experience. . . . At once unsettling and intimate. . . . *A Bad Character* is an astounding book: read it with the scent of diesel in your nostrils and red dust in your mouth."
—*The New Indian Express*

"A poignant and impressionistic portrait of the end of adolescence and a changing world."
—*The Telegraph* (London)

"Impressive in its . . . evocation of a dazzling, dangerous cityscape." —*Kirkus Reviews*

Deepti Kapoor

A BAD CHARACTER

Deepti Kapoor grew up in Northern India and attended college in New Delhi, where she worked for several years as a journalist. *A Bad Character* is her first novel. She lives in Goa.

A
BAD
CHARACTER

A
BAD
CHARACTER

a novel

Deepti Kapoor

Vintage Books
A Division of Penguin Random House LLC
New York

FIRST VINTAGE BOOKS EDITION, NOVEMBER 2015

The Library of Congress has cataloged the Knopf edition as follows:
Kapoor, Deepti.
A bad character : a novel / Deepti Kapoor. — First United States edition.
pages   cm
1. Teenage girls—Fiction.   2. Delhi (India)—Fiction.   I. Title.
PR9499.4.K3763 B33 2015
823'.92—dc23   2014020809

Vintage Books Trade Paperback ISBN: 978-0-8041-7133-5
eBook ISBN: 978-0-385-35275-8

www.vintagebooks.com

Printed in the United States of America
10 9 8 7 6 5 4 3 2 1

A
BAD
CHARACTER

My boyfriend died when I was twenty-one. His body was left lying broken on the highway out of Delhi while the sun rose in the desert to the east. I wasn't there, I never saw it. But plenty of others saw, in the trucks that passed by without stopping and from the roadside dhaba where he'd been drinking all night.

Then they wrote about him in the paper. Twelve lines buried in the middle pages, one line standing out, the last one, in which a cop he'd never met said to the reporter, He was known to us, he was a bad character.

It's a phrase they use sometimes, what some people still say. It's what they'll say about me too, when they know what I've done.

Him and me,
   (long dead).
   Sitting in the café in Khan Market the day we met, in April, when the indestructible heat was rising in the year, sinking in the day, the sun setting very red, sacrificing itself to the squat teeth of buildings stretching back round the stinking Yamuna into Uttar Pradesh.
   The city is a furnace on days like these, the aching heart of a cremation ground.

. . .

But inside the café you wouldn't know it; inside it's cool, the AC is on, the windows are politely shuttered, it could be any time of day in here; in here you could forget the city, its ceaseless noise, its endless quarry of people. You could feel safe.

Only he's staring at me.

Twenty and untouched. It's a sin. For twenty years I've been waiting for this one thing.

Idha.

In the mirror.

I give myself a name, I wear it out. Lunar, serpentine, desirous. A charm that protects me.

ONE

By the time I met him he was already gone. I didn't know it then, but he was gone. Because he never once paced himself, because he was racing forward from the moment of birth and every bridge he crossed he turned round to destroy. Chaos mixed with joy, the joy of Shiva, biting his mother's breast, madness in the blood.

And I couldn't have saved him; he wasn't there to be saved. Instead he picked me up in the café and tried to make me in his image. He said, You're my lump of wet clay. And it's true in a way, I was.

.   .   .

So now we're sitting in this café in Khan Market the day we met, in April, in the year 2000. In Khan where it's civilized, where there are bookstores and florists, and the music shop still selling cassettes, all joined together in a horseshoe and no big chain stores yet. Where the grocery shops for the embassy crowd are long and thin, with shelves packed high, full of imported goods, of Nutella and Laughing Cow cheese, Belgian chocolate and Spanish olives. Where the great and the good of Delhi walk upon the cracked pavements, or send their servants at least.

And in this café on the first floor, the waitresses are from the north-east, from Manipur and Assam. The tables and chairs are wooden, painted dark green, distressed like Parisian antiques. There are nooks and crannies in here to hide from the day, old posters on the walls, terracotta floors for the feet. They play Brubeck and Dylan on the stereo, brew filter coffee, bake carrot cake and serve toasted brown-bread sandwiches on large white plates.

People are returning to India these days. Money is pouring in from every hole. It's also rising up out of the ground, conjured from nowhere, a miracle of farmland and ruins, an economic sleight of hand. There's construction everywhere, in Defence Colony and GK they

are building, and out in the satellite wastelands of Gurgaon and Noida they are building cities too.

Laxmi is doing her job, for those who know how to pray.
    It's every man for himself.
    India is Shining.

But me, I've gone nowhere, done nothing.

I'm in the second year of college, in the care of Aunty.
Not in dorms, not in hostels, not with other girls, no,
there's no paying-guest house for me. No mother either
any more, and my father, he's off living in Singapore,
abandoned me a long time ago for a new life there,
though no one will say it out loud, though everyone still
pretends it's not the case.

No, I'm alone, in college, living in east Delhi over the
filthy Yamuna, in the care of Aunty. My mother grew up
with this woman, who I can never call by name. She went

to school with her too, and then was left behind. Aunty is a proper woman, she will be until the day she dies.

So I go to college and I come back home, I sit with Aunty in front of the soaps or else study and daydream in my room. But sooner or later I'm always called outside to be presented to whichever visitor has dropped by, or else I'm dragged with Aunty on one of her endless visits, to sit in other apartments and living rooms with the other aunties of this world, their daughters too sometimes, listening to the incessant talk about other lives, their weddings, sons and daughters gone astray, the ones who have failed, the servants who will not do what they're told, the property disputes, scandals, jewellery, the price of gold. I keep my head down here and my thoughts to myself.

I have my classmates in college of course. Not quite friends but they're still nice girls. With them I go to the movies sometimes, and sometimes we sneak out to TGIF to get a Long Island iced tea or a beer and sit around the table talking about the films we've seen, the clothes we've bought, the boys at college we're supposed to like, the ones we dream of marrying, besides the film stars.

.   .   .

Once or twice I've even had dates with these boys, been to coffee shops nearby and listened to them talk. They're such good bright boys that I should be in awe, but on these dates I'm always left cold. I sit as they talk and feel nothing for them, and the world keeps turning, but no one knows what turns in me.

Then, driving home to Aunty in my car, round the monumental grandeur of India Gate, across the black water of the creeping Yamuna, a pain grips my heart. My father bought me this car at the start of college's second year, out of guilt perhaps, or as a consequence of his new wealth. But driving home a pain grips my heart and I put my foot down to speed in the sulphurous dark.

There's another girl in the flat across from me. In the window of the tower block along the void of empty air I see her sometimes looking out. She's my shadow self, I decide. I keep a watch for her and then write foolish words about hope and love in my diary before I sleep.

. . .

And before waking each morning I dream. As the light breathes into the city I am leaving again: instead of the library I make my way north, along the river's edge towards the iron railway bridge, joining the Ring Road and driving up the Grand Trunk Road, leaving the city, going all the way to Chandigarh. Beyond Chandigarh there are the wheat fields of Punjab and the foothills and mountains that rise above. I drive through them to places I've never seen, that only live on these maps of mine: Mandi, Kullu, the Rohtang Pass, the east Ladakhi plateau, into the void above where nothing more exists.

But even in dreams I don't make it. In my dreams I am stuck on the edge of town, with the sun coming up around the Yamuna pipelines, the shredded prayer flags of the Tibetan refugees, the swampland near Model Town, where everyone is shitting and brushing their teeth on the side of the road, running for the buses in the shimmer of exhaust fumes bouncing off the heat of baking stone.

I climb out of bed into the cold of the AC to look at myself in the mirror, my black eyes and my pale cheeks, and I wait for this one thing to happen to me.

I run.

I run a lot in these college days, in the colony below the tower block, in the faded little park where the aunties go for their morning strolls, after the cleaners have swept the rooms and the cooks have been given their work. It's the same park where the servants sit on the benches during their breaks, trading house gossip and complaints, and where the drivers lie wolf-eyed, waiting to be called in the shade. I run a lot in this park in the mornings, before all this happens, and in the evening before the sun goes down I run too, put on a CD and just run. Going in circles because the park is so small, listening to Moby in the beginning—simple, uplifting, driving my feet forward. And then later listening to the trance my love gives me, hard, dark and hypnotized.

But before all this I listen with bursts of hope, desperation, burning up the energy that has nowhere to go. I want to run in the night, to get up at 4 a.m. and go out into the deserted lanes, charge down the middle past the sleeping dogs, over the potholes. I wake up in the dead of it and listen to the AC and I want just to put my music on and go out there, make my lungs burst, and run. Only Delhi is no place for a woman in the dark unless she has a man and a car or a car and a gun.

*

But now we're in this café, a place I visit often. I drive a little, then I come to sit, to read a book, to pretend to think. I chat with this waitress of mine, this Chinky, as Aunty calls her, this woman from the north-east. She's very beautiful to me, but we only talk between orders, in the time she takes to collect my cup and plate, and even then she lingers with one foot ready to leave, an ear cocked to the rest of the room. In snatches she tells me about her troublesome brother in Manipur, her loving husband who is educated and too proud to take on lesser work. Around her eyes she wears a thick ring of kohl to make them seem larger—she says quite sadly that she has small eyes, that they're ugly, but I like her eyes, as I like everything about her: alert, mournful, intelligent, but most of all different. And while the kohl around her eyes looks like rebellion, around mine it is a prison.

Once or twice in my green bathroom light have I put kohl around my eyes like hers, thickly, admiring them.

But she's not here today.

And across the room he is staring at me.

. . .

I've been stared at a lot, of course; it's what happens here, it's what men do. Every day, from door to door, on the buses, stepping through rubble on the edge of the road, in the car stuck in traffic, at red lights. Stares of incomprehension, lust, rage, sad yearning, so vacant and blank sometimes it's terrifying, sometimes pitiful. Eyes filling the potholes, bouncing down the street like marbles, no escaping their clank. Eyes in restaurants, in offices, in college, eyes at home. Women's too, disapprovingly.

But in his eyes there's the promise of something else.

*

So I'm in this café in Khan Market, twenty years old and I'm beautiful, though I only know it now looking back at the photos I have of myself, where it's obvious, painfully so because it's gone, this beauty, never to return, where the skin is so young and unmarked by life, still with the last traces of puppy fat, but how deep is the hunger in the eyes, the joy right there inside her at the moment she's being shaped and devoured.

.   .   .

And nobody knows, nobody will. That's the thrill of it. None of my classmates, no family. They'll know something is up, that something has changed, but if they knew for certain what it was, if they could see him, they'd be horrified beyond belief, because he's ugly.

Ugly with dark skin, with short wiry hair, with a large flat nose and eyes bursting out on either side like flares, with big ears and a fleshy mouth that holds many teeth.

There's something of the animal in him. Something of the elephant and the monkey. Something of the jackal.

He's not a typical "Delhi boy," that's for sure, not only because of his face and skin but also because of the clothes he wears: a faded yellow T-shirt that's been washed too many times, a pair of too-large brown corduroy pants held up with an old belt. A vagabond who's been scrubbed clean. But there are also brand-new red Converse sneakers on his feet, with their clownish white rims that tell me he's not exactly from the street.

He's nothing like the boys they want me to marry. There's a new one of those on the horizon, a nonresident Indian, twenty years in the U.S., a full-blooded American now. Aunty is lining him up for a meeting. I sit with her at home on the sofa while she tells me all about him. She leafs through his biodata, his golden résumé, and in this apartment high up in the air I cannot breathe. I eat and sleep but I cannot breathe. She's been arranging these meetings for a year now, without success, but she never tires, and this new one is very promising to her: he's seen my photo and approved of my looks, and because he's divorced he's willing to overlook my own unfortunate situation, the mother dead, the father absent.

Aunty doesn't imagine I'd ever say no, and after so many rejections, after so many families have turned me down, she's giddy about this one.

Sitting on the sofa. Listening to her speak. The soap operas on the TV, the thick curtains drawn, the fan spinning dead air. Such heavy furniture in her world, stared at by that dark wood, by those statues of gods, by bronze and dried fruit, by nuts tied in packages with bows, left over from this wedding or that, from Diwali.

Uncle is in his bedroom looking through the accounts,

or pretending to at least, drinking his peg of whisky. His world is his own, he doesn't share it with me—only good morning, how are you, fine, off to college, very good. Never any emotion, no affection for his wife, not in public at least. Only the motions of putting food on the table, only off to the factory or the club and then to sleep.

In front of the TV Aunty looks at me sadly. She sees my stubbornness, my lack of enthusiasm, and suddenly she's afraid for me.

But I'm actually considering the American, that's the truth. I'm seriously thinking of saying yes to him. I've been toying with the idea for a while now. The neighbour says, But he's divorced, and Aunty says, So what if he's divorced, he's learned his lesson, he makes good money, he's a good family boy, what more is there? And unlike this one in the café, the American is not ugly at all.

It's the years of conditioning that make me think his dark skin is ugly, poor, wrong. That make me think he looks like a servant.

.   .   .

But in the café I'm looking up at him.

I am pretty and he is ugly.

And the secret is this turns me on.

*

I tried many times to write this down, and all have failed. Ten years gone by. Words deleted from hard drives, set on fire in ditches, in metal bins on balconies, pages torn up in frustration, scrunched into balls and tossed away. I tried to write this down but went about it the wrong way. How to write while being pursued? When one is not the pen but the page?

*

So, Varanasi, aged eight. Still in pigtails, wearing my tartan dress. Still a little mute and pensive, my lips pursed, looking in the mirror but not quite recognizing myself, not yet comfortable in my own skin. I want to be grown-up more than anything, but for now I'm only aware enough to be embarrassed of myself. I don't know any other way; I certainly don't know how to change it. It doesn't occur to me that it's within my power to change anything, to make decisions of my own. So I'm stuck in this body and the clothes I'm given to wear. But it's also true that I like my tartan dress.

Varanasi, my father: the last time I remember you whole. As if you were a thing that could be broken apart, like a chocolate bar.

We went together, the three of us, mother, you and me, a final holiday. You were back from Singapore, the last time before you left for good. We took the train from Agra and stayed with relatives in the old city, near the Ganga, in a house in a tangle of lanes with a courtyard inside that one would never know was there.

This lane is so narrow we have to press ourselves against its sides as the bodies come by. They come as torpedoes wrapped in cloth on the hands of sadness towards the Ganga to burn.

He once told me, he said, Even after burning, the breast-bones of men and the pelvises of women remain. That instead of crumbling to ash they are sent down the river to sail, to sink in its bed. One day when the Ganga dries up they'll find them there. Thirty billion pelvic bones, thirty billion sternums. The history of the world in a watery grave.

And just his presence. Just his hand on my belly as we sleep, when he loves me. It lives forever.

Close your eyes, go to sleep.

It lives forever, the hand on my shoulder in the train on the way, in the compartment, hanging down from the top bunk. I look at them, my mother and my father, and he is stroking her hair. He is holding her in his lap like a little bird.

In the black and yellow of the taxi to the city we sit with our luggage stacked around us on the torn leather seats. Then, in the lanes that are too narrow for taxis, a cycle rickshaw, groaning under our weight. They're carrying the luggage on their heads the last bit of the way—my bag is on my head, I'm mimicking them. Lots of legs, and those sudden processions of the dead coming round each bend.

At the house where we're staying, the courtyard has water flowing in narrow channels around its edge and creepers in bowls that climb up the walls to the lattice-screen balconies on the first floor. The gates of the courtyard open to the alleyway. When they are closed, the city remains as noise coming through a blue square of sky, where toy kites fall and rise. There's a hospital nearby. You hear the cries of the patients in the morning, the hacking of phlegm in the throat that is the song of India.

Then one evening the wind changes and a thin layer of grey falls on the courtyard floor. It's the ash, someone tells me, coming from the burning ghat, the ghat of the dead.

*

In the café I get up to go to the bathroom, and in the cramped bathroom away from the AC, I feel the city crawling over me—as soon as I'm through the door it crawls through the window in squashed and malodorous heat. In thousands of horns and voices, in red dust. Night is falling, so the people are moving back out to the streets, bulbs are being switched on in the stalls, in the doorways. The retreating sun releases fragrance, incense, sewer smells, frying food, exhaust fumes. The minarets give their call to prayer, the rising swarm of their devotion telling us that God is great.

*

Early next morning I left to see the dead. Alone, no one knew I'd gone, snuck out through the alleyways, I was drawn to the river, somehow I knew where it would be. Coming round a corner on the cobbles to a slope running north-east, long like the slopes that boats are pushed down, but at the bottom before the water it's the inferno of Dashashwamedh.

There are two pyres in my head, maybe three. The third might be lower down, out of focus, but these two are raised up, clear in my mind, on abutments of concrete. Behind there is a wooden tower and around this many piles of wood, many different kinds, each more expensive than the last, each more fragrant, to mask the smell of burning flesh.

There's already a body roasting there, almost done, its family quietly accepting now.

This girl would have looked wide-eyed to anyone watching her. Transfixed, standing without words. The smoke changing direction without warning, billowing across her, pieces of ash running into her dress, sticking in her hair.

Bluest of blue skies, not a cloud within it, and already hot at 7 a.m., even without the raging fires whose ripples in the daylight are a thing to behold.

After a lull, a new procession begins, the body wrapped in bandages as in the alleyways, the pyre cleared, the ash and logs swept away, the last bone set to sail as the soul drifts up past the crows on the rooftops and the new pyre is laid. They are sobbing, the women, a group of women holding on to one another. One in the middle cannot be contained. At any moment she might break away, fall forward to embrace the dead man's face.

It has a moustache, a balding head. It is laid on the criss-crossed wood, the fire is lowered on a stick, pressed in underneath. It takes hold and quickly begins to spread. The hysteria of the widow stops and it seems as if the whole universe has held its breath.

I feel the heat of the flames against my skin, I cannot take my eyes away, I think that he'll jump out at any moment and run. But nothing happens like this. Instead the moustache zips out of existence like a magic trick, the eyes melt, the yellow layer of fat beneath his skin becomes exposed, it starts to sizzle and pop. Soon the bright white bone shows through. He is burning away; he's dead and he is disappearing again. The widow: I watch her watching this, not removing her eyes, and there's no mistaking that nothing exists in time.

Afterwards, alone, far downriver, in silence beyond all roar, a naked Aghori smears himself in cremation ash.

He pulls a corpse from the water to pick at the bones, to eat the sodden and putrid flesh raw. Many years later I'll see him again in the final face of the man I love.

It's only when he dies that I'll become the person he wants me to be. Only when he dies that I'll let go, sleep with other men, let them sleep with me. But right now he's alive, I'm twenty, untouched, and he's staring at me.

*

When I come out of the bathroom he's sitting at my table. He says some women had moved to take it, thinking it empty, but he'd stopped them, he'd given up his own instead. I don't know if it's true, but the appearance of the women there backs up his words. And here he is at the table, standing up, holding out his hand, looking into my eyes, saying, Pleased to meet you.

His voice is educated, frank, completely unexpected. There's a foreign lilt to it, as with those who've been to the American School. Very slight—he wears it like a set of summer clothes. As if it could go up in smoke.

.   .   .

But his body, his eyes, his entire way of being, makes me think of someone who's been lost at sea, lost for a long time, or else wandered out of the forest, as if he's been in the forest and learned something there.

There's not a shred of fat on him, it's all muscle and sinew, coiled eye and glacier bone, as if he's covered every inch of land, burnt off every strip of fat through breathing.

So now there's this wild animal dressed in human clothes, with a set of keys picked up from the table and a wallet stuffed full of rupee notes.

*

When I went back to the house from the ghat that day there was ash all over my body, all in my hair and in my clothes. I reeked of smoke. They'd been looking for me, my mother was panicking. She beat me, stripped me and scrubbed me clean, and I cried for an hour in her arms.

Varanasi looks like the scene of a plane crash in my sleep. Small fires are scattered about, seen from above, scattered on the banks where the debris still burns, where homes have been wiped out without warning, where bodies are strewn. Night falls in Varanasi and pockets of fire still rage from the blackness, their flames reach up to diminish the stars, spewing sparks into deep space, souls orbiting the terror of this world.

There are lingams everywhere in the Varanasi of my dreams. On top of every step, at every ancient corner turned. It's a virile city, teetering on the brink. And on the other bank it is barren like the afterlife.

The Ganga is a river that flows backwards in time.

*

In Agra, in our crumbling ancestral home, six years old. I'm the same person I was when I was six years old. The same fear, the same watchfulness, the same cowardice too, the same sense of doom. The same desire to jump over the edge.

I sleep next to my mother when Father isn't here. We sleep in that same big bed in the silent house, silent as soon as the fans are off, eerie beyond belief. She pulls me towards her, murmurs in her sleep, twitches like a cat dreaming, whiskers in the hunt on some imaginary breeze, stalking the grass over the hill when the sun goes down. She bares her teeth at the squirrels in the eaves, and then she cries, so sadly that I lie with my breath held, listening to her moan.

Sleep, the only time she's really awake, the only time she truly cries. I love her. She never cries like this in the day. Never pities herself or bemoans her fate, never knows what has become of her.

She liked to bathe me in the old days, took great care with it, and one day she sat me down on the cold metal stool, opened my legs, and pointed between them, then said, If a man ever tries to touch you there, an uncle or a servant or a cousin, anyone at all, you fight him off and you scream. You run. You don't let anybody touch you down there. That is the worst place in the world.

*

I'm still in pigtails.

I'm running through the fields in my tartan dress, the

one brought back from Singapore, which he said was Scottish.

And the thunder breaks inside the sky, like the crack of an old record player. Skips across the surface, clicks. Follows a pause by the peal, rumbles between clouds the way the belly sky rumbles, mourns and quakes. Belly sky of tectonic plate. Rupture and rent.

Rent the blackness, billow the sail, on a ship of ocean ink.

The rain pours down on to the fields.

From thunderous chest of sky, on to the page.

On to childhood, my love.

A cadaver.

A labourer dead in the long grass. The sack of a cat from the side of a well, a rat killed by dogs in the short grass.

. . .

And in the house down the street they had a son.

So they lit fireworks.

They lit rockets and crackers and bombs.

Smoke on the ground blowing into our yard, because they had a son.

In the bedroom he puts his fingers between my legs. But in the café he tells me he's been living in New York, that he's only just come home, back to Delhi for good.

And do I like Chinese food? Yes, I do.

And do I have a car?

I have that too. Yes, I have a car.

Perfect, he smiles, drumming his fingers on the table, Then let's go, you and me right now. I'll buy you dinner, I know the place.

He looks me in the eye. This is how it starts.

*

In school we practise kissing one another. Take turns, giggle, watch in the bathroom mirrors, in the mirrors we make ourselves cry, cry and hold one another like our sons have died.

. . .

We walk home in our uniforms at the end of the day, and I dread walking home, I dread walking to school. I'm never good enough anywhere. I'm awkward. I carry it along with me into adulthood.

When I get my marks in class, I'm asked by the family where the other marks have gone—I'm compared unfavourably to the cousins with higher ones, the ones pegged for success, for government jobs, set to become doctors, lawyers and accountants. Only my English teacher believes in me. She tells me I have it in me to go all the way: to college, abroad, to be anything I want. To be a modern woman. That's what she says. Our headmistress says it too; in assembly she tells us we're what the country needs. You're the future of India, she says.

I look back on this childhood as if standing on the far bank of a fast-flowing river, impossible to bridge. And he is cutting through it, a drowning man in the dark waters of the monsoon.

*

The sun has gone down completely now. The noise of the city rises as it falls, she can't separate it from the heart-beat in her throat, the chattering of her teeth, because something is finally happening to her.

The guard at the door salutes him and they share a word. They're friends already it seems. He has a habit of this, she'll discover—of making poor people love him; he could raise an army of them if he wanted to, they think he's one of them in disguise. He offers her a cigarette and she declines, so he lights it for himself and asks her if she knows how beautiful she is, asks as if he's wondering what to do with it, as if it's a quality he might apply to a task. Then he laughs to himself and moves on, changes the subject, tells her that his car is over there and that they can meet across the lights towards Lodhi. He'll be waiting on the side of the road, he's got a red Maruti Zen with a sticker saying PRESS on the rear window in big letters. You can't miss it.

. . .

It's in the car away from his eyes that she thinks this might be madness, that it could be a trap. That this could lead to something untoward. The coward in her rises up and says that she should drive out the other way and go home, away from this strange man, never to come back, never to see him again, to keep living the life that Aunty preserves. But then she remembers home, Aunty and all of that, and she thinks how long she's been waiting for something to happen to her, how long she's been motionless inside herself. And now here it is, here's her chance. It might never come again.

*

Like my mother, I'm a loner. I'm sitting by the river near the banyan tree in Agra, she is calling out to me from the house at dusk, my father's ancestral home on the edge of town. He's still out working in Singapore but he'll return, he hasn't abandoned us quite yet. I hear my mother calling but I don't reply. She's fearful, imagining all the terrible things that can happen in the dark.

. . .

When he comes back he holds me in his arms. He smells of cigarettes. Of Old Spice aftershave and whisky. When he comes home he acts like nothing's changed.

My mother, she's suddenly awake, she's been nervous for days, cleaning the house, getting everything into shape for his arrival. She fixes her hair and puts on her best sari and thinks everything will be OK. When he turns up he brings gifts, all the latest electronic goods, kitchen things. They put on a big party for him—the family lays out all kinds of food on a long folding table, they put out the drinks in plastic cups, they blow up balloons, and everyone comes to meet him. He likes the crowds, my father, he likes the parties, he's a natural showman—handsome, a charmer. He shows off some magic tricks. I stand in the room watching him, watching my mother waiting. Now and then he passes by and runs his fingers through my hair, and when he puts me on his shoulders I hold him tightly, smell the Brylcreem with my eyes closed.

When the food is finished, the music played, when everyone has drifted back home, he takes my mother into the bedroom, he pulls her by the arm. I recognize that look on her face. He doesn't go to sleep when they're done, he watches TV in the living room and I slip out my door to crawl beside his chair. He never sends me back to bed. Instead we watch TV together for hours, until I've fallen asleep. In the day when there's no one there I go and lie on their bed, dwarfed by it as my mother is, watching the folds in the sheets turn into vast mountain ranges, tracing the caravan through the passages, laden with Arabian gold.

He's gone as quickly as he came, the thief.

Later I learned of his own father, my grandfather, the godman. He ran away too when he was young. Barefoot from village to village performing miracles, reciting the ancient texts by heart, sometimes speaking in tongues. From where he learned these no one knows. I met him several times when he was already old, but I understood nothing of him then, and by that time God had already left him in the corner of the room, like a lamp without a bulb, gathering dust.

*

It's the first year of college and the pleasant shadows of dreams have been banished by the spotlight of Aunty's world, where everything is good and right and clean. In this world there are no moments to yourself, for what's the need? Why do you need to keep your door closed? What are you hiding in there? It makes no sense at all to Aunty, this simple demand from the girl to please be left alone.

No, she's expected to be the same as them, to smile the right way, to say the right things, to be grateful at all times, to be seen and not heard. She sees this very clearly, in cars, in apartments, in homes, in pujas, in the same words and ritual learned by rote.

It's in this desperate life of preservation that death is held. Holding on to life only to die unblemished, to make it to the end, untouched by sin. And for what? What then? The girl sees this, and yet there's nothing to be done, nowhere to go. Nothing for her to do but grit her teeth, calm the voices inside.

. . .

Aunty knows the resistance in her, her reluctance. She chides her for it, calls her a snob sometimes. Says she only wants the best for her, that's why she says these things, because she cares. But she can't understand the behaviour of this girl.

On Diwali night she talks to me, after a rare drink, on the balcony watching the fireworks. The freezing shawl of smog envelops the city, makes the explosions flash like the synapses of a dying brain.

She says wistfully, In college your mother was a shy girl, a person I would describe as too shy, too quiet, a good girl, too sweet, everyone was very fond of her, everyone wanted her to do well. But every so often she would shock us with some strange words, she would say something completely unexpected, which took us all by surprise. She really lived with her head in the clouds.

She smiles apologetically, clears her throat, tugs her dupatta over her heavy breasts. From the balcony we watch the sky on fire and the city bombarded with light.

She gets nostalgic; she says, Life has been good to me. I've had all the advantages in this world. I've married well. I planned ahead. I have security now, though I've had my setbacks like anyone else. But you cannot just run and play in this life, you can't live on air alone.

She's only thinking of me, she says. I'm too young to understand, too much like my mother still. But my situation is precarious. Marriage is important. It needs to be handled well. One stray step and well, let's not talk about that.

It wasn't for love that my parents married. They were placed together in their awkwardness, in their deficiencies, through the taint of their blood, though it was known he was very handsome and she was oddly beautiful in her own nervous way.

My mother, who makes me read books. Who forces them on me, even as she drowns in loneliness, superstition, gossip and boredom, like so many good housewives before her. And not just any books, but the classics: works of great literature. There is a whole series in the library. We go through them together, one by one. She doesn't even know what's inside them, never reads them herself, just forces them on me the way another mother forces diamonds down her daughter's throat before the soldiers knock at the door.

*

In Bombay I hold her hand. I hold my father's too on the local trains, hold on for dear life. He says if either of us lets go then that will be it, the beggars will have me, they'll cripple my legs and send me to work.

Technicolor Bombay, that crack of hope, the heartbreaking city, clinging to the edge of India, falling off the century like a cartoon. We lived there awhile, not even a year—my father was posted from Agra for work.

When we moved my mother was happy at first, it breathed new life into her. There was that rotting fish smell, the salt of sea in the air, the trawler stench, the song of gulls, the relentlessness of jet planes taking off. It all held a breezy promise Agra never could.

. . .

In Khar West, it was an apartment building on the fourth floor, not the Delhi kind, not a mausoleum like Aunty's but bright and crumbling, open to noise; you could hear the others, their music, their TVs, their arguments; everyone on top of everyone else, palm trees growing up past the windows, coconuts ripening and crows swaying on the branches like happy drunks. Often I forget we lived there at all, it's a punctured dream of glossy print, clothes drying out on the balcony lines, blood oozing through Konkan saris in my sleep.

She dresses my hair with a Minnie Mouse bow and sends me outside to play with the other girls. Instead I climb to the roof to watch the ocean beyond the bald heads of the apartment blocks and the planes taking off in the haze.

I wait for Sunday all week. My mother is holding my hand on the way to the chicken shop with the money for the evening meal. It's so sunny here. The meat is hanging in great mean lines on the hooks, and scattered behind there's the scene of blood. Terrified, fascinated, I wait all week to see this flesh being chopped, but I pull away, almost close my eyes to it, when it comes. She buys one whole chicken, has it wrapped in paper, and at home she prepares it lovingly, with great concentration, with her tongue peeking out the corner of her mouth and a beatific look on her face. When we sit to eat in the evening, I'm amazed by the alchemy of this, the life made out of death.

There's a birthday party in the building one day and the girl whose birthday it is, her mother has told my mother I'm invited. And she's very excited, my mother, eager for me to go and be with the other girls, to dress up and play. I want to go too, to be accepted, to be with everyone else and adored.

So she bathes and dresses me. She puts me in a red dress with blue satin panels and ties a ribbon in my hair. Then I'm pushed out into the corridor and sent downstairs. But I never make it inside. I stand outside for an hour or more, unable to bring myself to knock on the door. When other people come by I run away and hide, pretend to be busy with something else. Eventually I escape to the roof. I cannot bear it, can't explain it either. The agony of being alive, of functioning like a human being. Can you understand this? This is who I am.

.   .   .

When I come down from the roof my mother is excited. She wants to know how it was, wants every detail of it. And I lie, I tell her it was wonderful, I had such fun, I made many friends. She's so happy for me.

But later she hears the truth from one of the mothers downstairs. She defends me at first, says it's a lie, I went there. And the woman says, I don't know what's wrong with that girl of yours.

Father comes home to find her howling in a corner, me hiding in my room.

*

I'm eleven years old. Back in Agra, full of rage. But only with my mother do I show it. Twenty years old and nothing's changed. Only the voice for it has been misplaced.

Twelve, looking through a friend's brother's porn smuggled in from abroad. He's hidden them behind the cupboards though we know where they are. *Playboy, Penthouse,* we look through them giggling, pretending to be ashamed. But I sneak one home and read it by torchlight under the sheets. I like the letters pages best of all.

*

Now it's night in the car. Night falls so fast here. From dusk it's only a heartbeat away, a curtain that falls into place. The songbirds give their final note, giant bats flit between the trees, perforating the sky. We are driving through the wide boulevards of Lutyens' Delhi, the colonial sweep of classical bungalows housing memories of order and rule, of radial roads and white cupolas shaded by tunnels of trees. Jasmine blossoms blow along the wind, the gulmohar glow like cinders. In the darkness I follow his tail-lights. He drives fast and then he coasts along, waiting for me to catch up. It's a game to him. He heads through Lodhi Estate, where the rich and powerful crouch in their mansions, their guards poking guns from their nests at the street. It's still very hot, a dry heat that sees men out everywhere on the grass, lit by the street lamps on the circles, in the scattered parks— men who've been stunned into torpor now stirring to put away their cards, light beedis, make fires, their bicycles propped up against the trees, some walking again. Women glide along the road, apart, single file, carrying babies, with baskets on their heads, impossibly erect, draped in frayed saris bright as Gauguin fruit. But none of this exists to me now, I can never be part of it, there's only his tail-lights ahead of me. I follow them down into south Delhi, all the way to Vasant Vihar, no longer alone.

I'm always alone.

I'm thirteen years old.

My breasts are puffing up like crisp little puris, the blood flowing out of me so hard I think I'll die. My stick of a body ripens, tightens, becoming newly curved. The flesh around my eyes takes on the purple of a bruise.

Such a spurt of growth that my clothes don't fit me any more. And I can never again wear my tartan dress.

Around this time my extended family becomes secure, finds wealth. My father's brothers, all moving forward in the world. Not spectacularly, not extraordinarily so, but more than enough to survive. The economy is opening up. Jobs are found. Land is bought and sold. Then come the cars, the washing machines, the televisions, the cousins sent off to America to study, to become doctors, accountants, lawyers and bankers. All the bases are covered.

But we do nothing, go nowhere. Though my father still sends money, we are displaced, shoved aside. I keep my head down in school and get lost in my dreams, but my mother sits outside it all, the exile, watching the rest of them in silence in the frozen halls of our home, becoming suddenly old, her hair getting tangled in knots. She removes her bangles. She doesn't sit with the other women, she only sits by herself and smokes. She has her suspicions, she laughs bitterly, as if someone has made a cruel joke about the world.

When I'm seventeen she dies. It's a short illness, there's no time. She's blown away like dust on the veranda wind. My father returns for the cremation. But they don't let me see her, and he doesn't take me back to Singapore with him. I don't know why it happens. I can't explain why I've been abandoned this way.

*

I'm avoiding him, that's the truth. Avoiding coming to him, knowing that as soon as I do he will reach his end. And my mother, my father, my family—perhaps there's no link to them at all.

*

Now the Delhi streets are sulphur and dead, the streets are bridled by fear. We go into Vasant Vihar, to sit in the Chinese restaurant, to smoke and eat chicken and drink beer.

Inside, the restaurant is red and gold; outside in the colony nothing stirs. The market is deserted except for the liquor store from which men scurry like rats with their twenty-rupee bottles of Doctor's Choice, before vanishing into the darkness of doors. Crumbling dead Delhi, gasoline ghost town in the dark.

In the restaurant the waiters know him. They welcome him with their watery eyes and obsequious grins. They wear grubby waistcoats and bow ties. They show us to a booth at the side of the room.

. . .

I say I shouldn't be here. She'll be waiting for me.

Who will? He offers a cigarette. I decline.

Aunty. Where I live.

Aunty . . .

Yes.

Where do you live?

Over the river.

And your parents?

My mother's not here. She's dead.

And your father?

In Singapore.

He nods to himself, smiles slightly, sympathetically. Lights his cigarette. Settles into the red booth.

What's it like in Singapore?

I say I don't know.

He flags down the waiter and orders two beers.

*

At home, Aunty would take me on her visits. For two years I'm dressed in my itchy salwar-kameez, sitting next to her juddering flesh, among the bags of clothes that are going somewhere, to be altered, to be gifted to someone else on the way, given away second-hand, untouched. This is the currency we trade in here, a great merry-go-round of unwanted gifts. The driver is looking at me through the rear-view mirror. He can't help himself. He positions it so he can see me instead of the road. But what to do? Aunty doesn't believe me when I complain, and the two of them, they're as thick as thieves. We're going round to Karol Bagh today, but first to Paschim Vihar. So many people to see. So many visits to be made.

During Aunty's visits I'm often asked what it is that I am studying, then asked what, with this, I can hope to achieve. An MBA would be the smart option, one uncle says, or accountancy. And though education is a good thing, it's true, it has its limits, just like freedom. Freedom and education, neither are to be abused, both should know their place.

And what about your marriage? Have you found someone yet? Aunty sighs and shakes her head. Then perking up, she talks about the NRI.

But today they discuss the servants, how they're all controlled by their maids. How they're slaves at their mercy, held ransom to their whims. I keep my head down and try not to think.

In college, in my lectures, it's much the same. I write words but I've lost interest in what they mean. The lecturers don't seem to care themselves; the students seem only to repeat what they're told.

I have my own ideas about things and a couple of times, having coffee with the girls, I've ventured some thought close to my heart only to receive blank looks in return.

But I'm twenty and really there's nothing wrong with my life. I have everything a girl could want or need, a modern girl like me.

*

In the restaurant I take one of his cigarettes. He lights it for me.

It's starting to fill up inside. All around there's the stench of cooking, the MSG, the smell of stale carpets, ashtrays, empty glasses, the stickiness of beer on plastic floors, the warm aroma of chicken and noodles and red chilli, the soy and turmeric that comes all the way from the Chinese of Calcutta, the gobi Manchurian that crowns their hard work far from home. The noise is a womb, waiters are shouting to the kitchen, the kitchen is sizzling in white light behind the swing door. On the wall in the corner there's a cricket match on TV. Every now and then the waiters stop in clusters to watch a replayed shot, a wicket, drunken men shout at a decision. Out on the open floor around the big round tables people are drinking, arguing, stuffing their faces, making deals. Lots of cheap white-shirted businessmen in here, lots of Punjabis, Taiwanese, Malays, Chinese.

He asks what I'm doing exactly. I tell him, literature. When he asks why, what's the reason behind it, I hesitate and he sees this and says it's just a question, not a trap, he only wants to know what I think. I tell him that I don't know why. Because it's the only thing I was ever good at. I tell him about my mother and her books. But I say I hate it now. It's nothing like what I thought it would be.

What did you think it would be?

I shrug. I don't know.

What are you going to do about it?

A pause. I don't know.

He smiles. You don't know much, do you?

I must look hurt. He corrects himself, says he's joking. It's just a joke. He understands how I feel. Then he asks what I'd really do, if I could do anything.

A simple question, but again I don't know. There's a moment of silence where I feel nervous, and to fill it I blurt out, like a confession, that I'm stuck, that they all want to get me married off, but I don't want to get married at all.

He lets this sit between us and I think right away how I shouldn't have given so much, because I can't be sure of him, I have to remember this, though already I want to trust him, already I want to tell him things. He looks at me out of his large, dark eyes. I've been starved of this look for so long.

The waiter comes to take the order. He orders chilli chicken, Hakka noodles, veg Manchurian, fried rice, two more beers. You have an accent. I say this when the waiter is gone. He leans back in the booth and smiles. He must know that it's part of the reason I came with him, the security it brings. It marks him out as different too. Combined with his ugliness, his confidence, his dark skin, it's intriguing. For someone who looks like him, it turns him into a mystery.

It's from New York, he says. I picked it up there.

You lived in New York?

He nods. For seven years.

How old are you now?

Twenty-eight.

I put the cigarette out, push the ashtray away and sip some beer.

What's it like in New York?

He says, Why, would you like to go? It's too bad but it's too late, I'm already here, otherwise I'd have taken you, shown you around, it would have been my pleasure.

From across the table I can smell his aftershave and suddenly I feel cold. We're next to the AC. I see the hairs on his arms standing on end, and the thin, faded T-shirt he wears, washed so many times that now the threads show.

*

New York was the making of him. It was the place where his ideas took flight. First he studied film, later psychology. He pursued journalism on and off in between, worked in a restaurant, in a record store. It's all connected. It's one and the same.

But he says it wasn't the lecture halls that did it for him. Instead it was the streets. In the streets he could see it all quite clearly, walking around the Lower East Side, Chinatown, SoHo, Washington Square in the winter sun, freezing cold, up Fifth Avenue, the skyscraper canyons so vast they cut out the glow, the razor air splitting your lungs. Through the park, through Columbia, round into Harlem. He realized here he could be anyone.

He suddenly talks about the light there. He says the light in the winter in New York is beautiful, it's so thin. It's nothing like the Indian light, which is heavy and dull, full of dust, involved with the gods. Their light has no gods, only Weegee, Trocchi and King Kong.

He tells me about Chinatown too. Bubble tea, dumplings and pork buns, about the escalators to get into the restaurants, the revolving tables in the giant banquet halls. How easy life is there. About Washington Square and Harlem jazz beyond the park. Do I like jazz? Do I know Mingus and Coltrane? He'll play them for me.

If it's so good, why did you come home? He inhales the question, taps his cigarette slowly, exhales smoke, looks at me as if deciding what to say. After a long time he tells me that it's because both his parents died, they died together in a car crash on Mathura Road. On the way back from a wedding party late at night, a truck from Haryana came on to the wrong side, the driver was drunk or asleep, they never knew. But he veered across at a junction and ploughed straight into them. There was nothing anyone could have done. They were killed right away. Of course the driver and his boy left the scene, absconded back to their native village, never to be seen again.

I tell him I'm sorry. I don't know what else to say. He shrugs and tells me it's all right, I don't have to be sorry, it's life and it was a year ago now, there's no more pain. Besides, I wasn't driving the truck, was I? So why apologize?

He describes them to me. They were doctors in private hospitals—a heart specialist and a paediatrician. Serious people, cautious, they never touched a drop of alcohol in their lives, didn't smoke, never went on holidays, never spent money on themselves. That's why they could afford to send him to New York, why he could stay so long there, spend so much money. They paid for his education, they paid for everything.

But now they're dead. He looks down and closes his

eyes for a second, tries to smile. He suddenly seems filled with regret.

I was the only child, he says. The prodigal son. I inherited it all, the money, the apartments, the ancestral land. I'll never have to work again.

He leans back and says, But that's not the real reason I'm home. In the end it's very simple: this is where the world is going. India's the future and America is done.

The food comes. The ashtray is full. The waiter takes it away. The waiters, they're all hovering in the wings, casting glances. They know him, he eats here often, but he says he's never been here with a girl before. Certainly never a girl like me. And now he's a conquering hero in their eyes. He looks around, he knows it, he's pleased. He says with satisfaction that he loves these places, the service, the food, the atmosphere, the sense of brotherhood one feels, the anonymity, the way they connect to the pulse of the city. He says he knows a thousand just like this, he knows them all, all over the city, he hunts them out, blends into them, he's a connoisseur of low-down dirty joints, side-street shacks, roadside carts, the best paratha, the best chicken, the best bad whisky, the best dal. The best dal of them all, he says, is on the Jaipur road, at one of the dhabas out there. Dal like you wouldn't believe. He drives on these highways in the night, all night sometimes, he drives to Jaipur and back when he can't sleep. He drives up and down the highways until the sun begins to rise.

We eat hungrily with the beer. Spill on to the tablecloth. I ask where he lives, he says in Nizamuddin West, close to the dargah, the tomb of the saint, at the point where the neighbourhood goes from rich to poor—he can sometimes hear the singing in the night, the qawwalis, the voices, the harmonium, the devotion filling the alleyways from the inside out. He says he'll show it to me some time.

He lives there alone, it's just him. No family, no flatmates, no maid, no cook, no servant. No prying eyes. No sentiments to offend.

I've never met anyone who lives alone, not once in my life. It's such a strange, alien thing, inconceivable in my world, where lives are piled on top of one another in a mass grave.

His apartment is being renovated now, he's fixing everything, but it'll be complete soon and then he'd like to show it to me.

. . .

He leans forward, offers another cigarette. And what about you? Tell me. He's very curious, he wants to know. What was I doing in the café? What was that look on my face? Where had I come from? Where was I about to go? He was watching me a long time before I saw him there. He couldn't help himself. There was something about me, something different, he knew it immediately, knew he had to speak to me, to know me somehow. I had a rare sort of power in me.

Embarrassed, I say I don't know about that. I came from college, that's all, I had nowhere else to go but home, and I didn't want to go home.

Do you go there a lot, to that café? I say I do, no one bothers me there. Not usually at least. He smiles apologetically. Did I bother you? I'm sorry. Do people bother you a lot? I bet they do.

We fall quiet, he's thinking about something. I say, Do you miss them? He looks at the table. Do I miss them, you mean my parents? He pauses, sketches a pattern quickly on the cloth. You know, when I heard they were dead it was evening in Manhattan. I was walking on Mulberry Street, north, through Little Italy, to Lafayette, up to Union Square, I had my set routes I liked to walk. There's nothing like walking there, you never tire of it. I was just walking, it was very cold, damp, almost snowing, and all the Christmas decorations had started to be put up around the city. I could see my breath in the air, and the noise when someone opened the door of a bar or restaurant seemed to flood the street with light. I was walking up towards Union Square when someone called, a relative, my father's cousin, I hadn't spoken to him in years. I hadn't spoken with my parents in a month. I kept walking as he spoke and then I stopped. He told me they were dead.

He stubs his cigarette out, lights another.

But listen, it wasn't grief I felt when I heard they were dead. Nothing like that. It was the most incredible feeling of a weight being lifted. It was a feeling of being free. Of being beyond judgement. Of course I loved them, but I was afraid of them too. Love and fear equally. Fear more than love maybe.

What I knew right then was that I'd never be afraid of anything again, I'd never be embarrassed or ashamed, I'd never have to hide. I could live my life exactly as I wanted.

Our eyes meet, they hold awhile.

And now I'm here in this city that I love.

I look down. I say I hate this city. I hate it here. All I want to do is leave.

He's surprised. He can't understand it. It seems unreasonable to him, short-sighted. Go where? He says he wouldn't trade it for anywhere else in the world. There's only Delhi. It has everything you need.

I tell him, That's easy for you to say. You went away, you came back, you saw the world first. You have money and you're a man. You can do whatever you please.

He shrugs and sits back and watches me.

Silence again.

And suddenly serious, leaning forward with his elbows on the table, he says, Let me show you. Let me show you the city then. See how good it can be. I'll be your guide. Make your mind up for yourself. Let's make a deal. He holds his hand out.

·   ·   ·

It's getting late. I say I have to go home, I'll be in trouble. He pulls his hand back and watches me with a long, indulgent smile. He says OK, I understand. But just think about it, I don't bite, and the offer still stands. He says he's grateful for the evening regardless. I took a chance on him and that's rare, he's thankful for it, most girls would run away, boring, normal girls, but I'm different, he was right about me.

Calling for the cheque, crumpled banknotes fall from his pocket, with them a pack of tissues, a pen, his battered silver Zippo. He scoops the money into a pile on the table, starts to pick through it, gives up, doesn't even count it properly, just sucks on his cigarette and throws money together into the mess in the middle. OK, he says, that should be more than enough. He stubs the cigarette out, drains his beer, puts the rest of his things away.

Outside it's dead quiet. The liquor store is shut, the market is as pleasant as a ruin. The heat is finally bearable too. We stand for a moment facing one another in the yellowing light and only now do I realize how drunk I am, but also how alert to him. I want to say something. I can't think of what it is. Instead he asks if I'm OK to drive. I say I'll be all right. He nods and tells me to follow his car as far as Jor Bagh.

Lodhi Road, opposite Safdarjung's Tomb, at the entrance to Jor Bagh, he pulls into the service lane at the side.

Nothing stirs beyond, inside the colony the gates of the small entry roads have been locked, the rich houses inside are packed up for the night, guards are in their cabins. A pack of stray dogs cross silently beyond us into Lodhi Gardens. We speak out of our windows. He says he wants to see me again.

When?

Tomorrow.

Tomorrow . . .

Tomorrow at noon, right here.

OK.

OK. He smiles. I'll be waiting. It was good to meet you. Think about what I said.

It's only when I'm free of him that I'm spinning out into space, racing back home as if I'm being chased in the fields, by the river with the barking dogs as the sun goes down, and my mother waiting for me inside.

*

I left Agra for Delhi in the middle of the monsoon, when the air was cool and sweet and teeming with life. Aunty sat with me in the train, outside we etched past the rubble bungalows of my childhood, past their fields of clothes lines with sheets already soaked by the sudden rain, falling in great drops, stinging when it hit, the noise it made on the blue tarp and tin of the slums drowning everything else. Rain on the grille, the cold air twisting through like a string of magician's silk. A note of thunder rolling through the vault of cloud, the wind rattling water through the trees. And my mother, left behind in the river and on the wind.

Inside the train people shifted, chattered, gorged themselves on food. North towards Delhi we went, past the rotten towns of dhabas and trucks, towns of mud, brick and kilns, towns of dogs and cows shaped in half-light, dirt-road towns with names like Tundla, like the names of vegetables I didn't want to eat. In each town

God's music grew louder, the music of horns and voices, loudspeakers and temple bells, like all the rivers coming together to pour into a chasm in the centre of the earth.

Now crows cry and dogs bark, the canopy of the day grows dim. Aunty is talking at me, telling me about her splendid college days.

She doesn't tell me about her own daughter though, the one who was born the same year as I, who died when she was four years old from childhood leukaemia caught late. Aunty sitting with her through the radiation, holding her hand, the doctors trying to keep her out of the room. They can't, she won't leave, she gives them no choice. But it doesn't matter because the treatment fails, and her hand is soon left on its own.

*

We entered the city late in the day, the train dragging along so slowly it seemed we were on the verge of a complete stop, where all the other passengers would just jump off and walk away. But we never stopped, we only crawled on.

. . .

And in New Delhi station the red-jacketed coolies dance among the crowds, piling luggage in their private rhythm, their teak-hard bodies absurd beneath the colour of their uniforms.

We are standing on the concourse beneath the white of the station light and the old ticking clock, Aunty uncomfortable in the crowd. We're sweating, waiting for Uncle to appear. He's corralled some coolies, now he's leading us over the footbridge, through a thousand bodies, until we've reached the end of it and climbed down to the earth, spat out at the rear of the station where whole villages sit with sacks and boxes, chain-linked together amid the rubble, waiting for something to come.

The sun has squeezed its last light into the sky. There is an overwhelming darkness that carries no breeze, which traps the city in an avalanche of heat.

. . .

Uncle leads us through the wreckage of the car park towards the car that is gleaming and beautiful save for the dent in its side and the young man with the sly body leering there. Uncle barks at him, he doesn't move at first, then he slides himself into the driver's seat and settles with a smirk. We climb in, the luggage is packed away, Uncle dismisses the coolies with some notes. The driver's eyes move over me as he reverses and I shift myself out of his gaze.

Past Delhi Gate, consuming blackness, splintered headlights through the scratched glass screen. The whine of monstrous buses pulling across the lanes. On the horizon factories ink their smoke into the deepening sky. Then driving out over the shrouded Yamuna, a demented pastoral scene in the river beneath, of medieval huts within the reeds.

We reach the other side, cross a busy junction. The first line of buildings gives way to a million more, the road lined with shops of all kinds, white lights selling kitchen appliances, clothing, sweets. The glow of hanging bulbs that crowd the pavement casts strange shadows on faces.

A crowd throngs around a temple; many hands surge up to reach the bell.

In east Delhi, through the thicket maze of streets, we turn to come to a road with a security booth and a guard holding a barrier attached to a rope.

In the colony, the houses press in on all sides, big blocks of Punjabi wealth, three storeys high, gilded with business money inside. The narrow road ahead is heaped with piles of sand where construction carries on. The car slaloms through to an open space where three faded tower blocks rise. At the foot of one, a gang of kids play with sticks. A mound of rotting garbage is dumped further to the side.

Inside the tower, the doors of the lift close, its thin metal walls pop and groan. On the walls lewd graffiti is scrawled in marker pen, on the floor paan stains look like giant mosquito kills. The lift doors quiver open on the tower's seventh floor. From the vacant square in the hallway wall the city shimmers north-east, the houses and slums forming a causeway out past Moradabad, running all the way out to Nepal.

Aunty's apartment is just like her body. Lacquered. The air inside barely stirs. Statues of gods everywhere, in brass, gold, wood, furniture of the darkest kind, thick red carpets on marble floors. Uncle pours himself a whisky and strolls into his room. The maid is frying onions in the kitchen, singing film songs. Outside you can feel that it's going to rain, a thunderstorm is coming, rattling the AC, making the pigeons babble nervously on the ledge.

She shows me to my room. It is long and thin, lined on one side with white plastic wardrobes. There is a desk and a bed and an old lamp, and just beside the bed a door into a bathroom of my own.

I sit on the bed for a long time. I press my palm against the window, try to connect it to the sleeping oven outside.

.   .   .

In the end I go into the bathroom, lock the door and close my eyes. Open them again in the weird medicinal light. When I look inside the mirror I see myself almost for the first time. Almost adult, almost there. On this monsoon evening all the electricity of the universe is in the sky. The storm outside is building very slowly, it won't break for hours. And the muezzins start their call to prayer, minaret to minaret, erupting in faith, along with the bleat of a train somewhere else.

The city is close to me now, I think I know it. Millions of lives, hearts, lungs, arms flailing and stabbing, begging, beating, pleading, praying, pushing gums against teeth, teeth against flesh, tongues lolling, bodies rubbing in the dark, drunk, fraying, frayed hems on clothing, loose stitches, goats, chickens, one great cry, the scent of it, the red dust and diesel in my nostrils and my mouth. I think I know it all. Then it ends.

Aunty walks through the door with the tea that's always cold. She says to hurry, the neighbours are coming, coming to meet me so put on my good clothes, pull my hair back off my face. There are so many people she wants me to meet. There's no time to lose.

Later that night, at dinner, she talks about the girl in the window, in the tower block across the way. She says she's locked up for days sometimes. That father of hers, he's a beastly man, he drinks and locks her away, the mother died of course, the son ran off and won't come back. He sends boys to get his liquor for him, gives them ten rupees to fetch it, it's shameful, they come back with those bottles, the little ones.

Uncle shakes his head in silent disgust.

Quarter bottles, domestic.

Did you ever hear of such a thing? I say drink is a curse, I really do. I tell Ranjan to take water with his whisky, but does he listen to me? No he does not, it's my fate to be ignored. It's a real shame, but it's how the world is these days, the modern world of course, the lack of morals. Well . . . just look at this city, look at him across the way, he's a drunk, that's very clear. His daughter too, no good will come of her. The way she stands in that window looking out at the sky with that moon-face of hers. Who wants to see a face like that? Better to keep your blinds down, don't pay any attention to her. But all in all, yes, it's a nice set of people here, a decent society, there's only this one black mark against character. But what to do? We're good people after all, and we don't like to complain.

*

Things I remember from the first year in Delhi:

Someone is saying his morning prayers, his voice is echoing off the tiles, as if he's in a bathroom, but he can't be. I don't know if he's above or below me, in the same building or not. Monotony, it lasts twenty minutes or more. I use each one of them. As long as his prayers continue I allow myself to sleep.

From another direction, every morning without fail, a man retching, dry-heaving, putting his fingers down his throat to remove the blackness that blows across the city at night; pranayama maybe, three or four times, regular spaces. Twenty seconds only.

. . .

I hear the horns of the trains in the deepness of night, but when the light comes up they're different, callous and shrill like cheap army bugles. Their noises collapse into the day. There's no pleasure on a train after sunrise.

The same car reverses at the same time in the morning, always around 6 a.m. The reverse gear plays a song: Happy birthday to you, happy birthday to you, happy birthday, happy birthday, happy birthday to you. Over and over and over. Amplified around the towers.

*

I went to a tarot reader too, went with the college girls. This lady had set up in one of the bookstores in Khan, people had heard about her, they started to talk, saying she was the real deal, not a fake at all. She didn't just tell you the good things, she told misfortune too. This is what caught my ear.

So we all go there, my classmates and I, and each girl takes her turn, coming out the other side with stories of marriage, academic success, minor setbacks, triumph in the end.

When I sit down across from her I'm surprised, because there's no theatre to her at all. She's tall, with long, flowing, white-tinged hair, kajal in her eyes, a red bindi, forty years old. She smiles carefully, asks me my name. It's only on revealing the cards that her smile begins to fade, replaced by a look of concentration first, then hesitation, until her expression is cold and fixed. She slows down, seems lost in herself. When it's finished she looks up as if someone new has sat down. She says, I'm sorry. She says nothing else for a while. Composes herself. Shifts in her seat. She says, almost to herself, I'm sorry, but I've not seen this before.

She looks at me again and takes hold of my hands, runs them between her fingers. Do you plan to go abroad? she says. I shake my head, I don't know. She says, Perhaps you should.

Why?

She tells me, It's better for you that way. Better you

leave India as soon as you can. You should get out of the country and never come back. Terrible things are in your cards. If you stay here only bad things will happen. If you stay here the cards say you will die.

I stood up and walked away and I never told anyone what she said, though I buried the words inside me where they lived on, like a splinter over which the skin has regrown.

*

Now Dirty Delhi. Ice cream in metal carts. Grapefruit, watermelon, cut open, surrounded by flies, packed in ice packed full of amoebic dysentery, held in the hands of boys with stunted nails at bus stops, holding them up to the window for a grubby note of exchange. Chunks of melting ice and the rind of fruit eaten by cows, dogs, rats, monkeys, rats the size of dogs. Exhaust fumes from the buses and the autos and the cars. From Indraprastha Power Station. Battered nimbu-pani carts, books on sale at the stop lights: *Mein Kampf, Harry Potter, Who Moved My Cheese?* Hijras with stubble flashing their comely eyes on the Ring Road near Raj Ghat, crows above the latticed balconies of Daryaganj, where they sell books on the pavements on Sundays and battered magazines, where they make juice in bright displays. Delhi, yes. Black bilgewater from every orifice.

*

The girl in the other tower fascinated my window dreams. Was she real? I couldn't tell. I didn't see her for a long time, didn't even hear her, and then I did. Sometime in the brief autumn of that first year I saw her moon-face looking out of the open window at the sky. As soon as she appeared she turned back round, the way someone turns when they're being called in a film. Then, like a new word you learn, I saw her often. And one day she was at the bottom of the tower, just as I was coming back from college. She was carrying a couple of saris in her arms, folded into their plastic sleeves, walking into my own block on some errand. It was strange to see her in the flesh and she didn't recognize me. She was wearing shades, big black plastic ones on a frozen face. We walked into the elevator together and I half smiled. She gave a half-smile in return, but it was almost withering in disdain, or at least that was how it felt. I was tempted to speak but what would I say? She kept the shades on, was wearing blue jeans, a black sweater, very pale, quite plump, straight black hair. We rode up the elevator in silence until she got out at the fourth floor.

I met her another day and she recognized me then. We were in the car park and she offered me a lift. Where was I going? To college, I said. She said she'd take me some of the way.

We sat in a wary silence at first. Then without warning she began to speak, defiantly, almost scornfully, she said, I know you, you live in the other block across from me, I've seen you. I see you sometimes in the window. You always look so sad. Then she said, Guess what? Don't you dare tell anyone. I'm going to run away. You'll see soon enough. But don't you dare tell anyone.

She tells me her story: her boyfriend loves her and she loves him, but he's an Old Delhi Christian and the families will never agree, will not even meet. So they're going to run away and start again, away from family, away from everything. They have a way out too. He's a chef in one of the five-star hotels, nothing special yet, right at the bottom, but he has talent. He can chop faster than

anyone she's ever seen. And a chef can get work anywhere, that's what he says. She says it's all arranged. He
knows an agent who specializes in these things. They'll
fly to Montreal. But before Montreal they'll go to Nige-
ria, to Lagos—it's a simple matter of passports, money,
visas and bending the rules.

When I say nothing in return she looks at me with that
bold eye of hers. You don't believe me? Well, what do I
care. As long as you keep your mouth shut. You better
promise. I promise, and we drive the rest of the way in
silence until she drops me off beyond the bridge.

*

He was there at twelve the next day, waiting as he said
he would be, the engine ticking over, exhaust fumes pad-
dling out over the scorched asphalt earth. No breeze in
the sky, only the motionless blue, and the roads were all
quite empty, stricken by the burning sun.

I pulled my car up behind his, sat for a moment, got out,
walked to the passenger side, knocked on the window.

Behind the blacked-out windows, in the AC cool, there's smoke around his head, curling in blue, the stereo turned up so loud you can hear it outside, playing Mozart of all things. He says it blows the cobwebs away.

Here he is with such a strange look on his face, fierce, almost tribal, caught unawares. Then a great smile breaks out, he opens the door and he asks if I want to go for a drive.

Inside, through the plastic blast of the AC, his car smells of cigarettes and aftershave. Lived in, a private domain, the inside of a brain. There are piles of books, computer journals, old copies of *Crime & Detective,* CD cases, junk food wrappers and printouts on the seats and on the floor. Throw them to the back, he says. Stuff them in the glove box, wherever, it doesn't matter. He doesn't apologize for the mess, doesn't care. Doesn't try to be proper. In the back of the car it looks like someone might have slept there. I ask half jokingly if he did and he says, No, not last night, but sometimes, when I'm too far gone. It's good to wake up sometimes and not know where you are.

.   .   .

I still have my misgivings about going off like this, about being alone here with him. He could be anyone, he could take me somewhere, hurt me. But more than this I have misgivings about his face, and what this means, the implication of the step I'm about to take, beyond which at a certain point I cannot return. The question of what it will finally say about me.

We're driving through Lodhi Colony, around Mehar Chand, on the way to Lajpat Nagar, skirting the top of Defence Colony. He knows all the shortcuts, the alleyways. He cuts through the middle lanes, through inside lanes hemmed in by houses with back walls that have no windows to see the garbage piles, through the veins and arteries, then out on to a familiar road to my delight. He takes pleasure in dissecting Delhi, carving it up like this for me. And suddenly, in this certainty of his, I don't feel afraid. It is as if I've slipped into another world, driving through a city unfurling like a tapestry, listening to Mozart's Piano Concerto no. 20 in D minor.

He asks how it was, getting home last night. I say I didn't realize I was so drunk. He nods and smiles. And how was this Aunty of yours? Did you get into trouble with her? I say I slipped in while she was watching her soaps, managed to get to my room and shower, change my clothes, brush my teeth, but came out to find her sitting on my bed sniffing the air.

I can just imagine it, he says. And what then? What did you do?

I'd told her I had gone for a movie with friends. She said I should have called her if I knew I was going to be out late, I know how she feels about me driving home in the dark.

Yes Aunty, I know, I'm sorry. You've told me a hundred times before, I must call, or don't even stay out at all, come back before the sun goes down. But I have to be out for college, and it's rush hour early on, I'd be stuck in traffic for hours if I drove back then, so it's better that I wait until the traffic dies. You don't drive yourself, so you don't understand.

She sighs and shakes her head and says, Oh, you know how I hate that car.

. . .

It's true that Aunty hates the car. At the breakfast table she says she doesn't like to think of me alone, being alone is a sure sign of trouble, it attracts attention, it's a provocation to some. And what if I were to break down? What if there was an accident? What would happen then?

There's some truth in this, I know. But the real danger is of being out of control.

And though I stay in the library sometimes and do what I'm supposed to do, sometimes I also drive.

Sometimes I drive to the Grand Trunk Road and think about the mountains beyond. Sometimes I drive towards the airport to see the planes taking off. Sometimes I park near Kamla Nagar or go down among the old colonial bungalows of Civil Lines. But parking does attract attention. It has its own problems. What is she doing there? What does she want? Is she a whore? Is she waiting for a man? At traffic lights, in the middle of a jam. Stuck behind cages of chickens stacked in the backs of tempos, waiting to be killed. They do notice me, these eyes, discovering I'm all alone in this city of meat and men.

And filling gas at the station the attendant strokes my hand when I hold the money out to pay. But still I drive around the city tempting fate, fingering the walls of the cell for the point at which it will break.

*

When we drive I ask him more about his life, about America and New York. He tells me about the cinema, the theatre, the galleries, the music he's discovered, the indie shows, the club scene. He describes the parts of the city; he walks me through the streets, peers across Manhattan from the top of the World Trade Center, from the Empire State Building, rides the L train to Brooklyn. He comes back to Fifth Avenue and the canyon walls there, blotting out the sun.

He tells me about something else, on Fifth Avenue, right by the Empire State Building. It's January and he's walking north, the crowds are at the crossroads, all starting to cross mechanically before the red of the traffic light, not waiting for the green man because there's no traffic to be seen on either side of the road. Both sides of the crowd are stepping forward, they're about to meet like two sides in war, when all of a sudden there's a terrible scream in the air, as if someone has been stabbed, so terrible that everyone stops in their tracks, the entire crowd freezes still. It's a bicycle courier riding right through the gap at full speed. His voice is the only thing that parted the crowd, his voice and nothing else, no pain, no knife, no gun. It was amazing, he says. It struck him right there, the certainty of the rider, the reaction of the crowd. How a crowd can be controlled. How the bike would have crashed if he'd failed.

Every day we meet like this. I skip college; I tell Aunty I'm in the library studying for my exams, but then we meet and we drive and we talk. We talk through everything that needs to be said. He asks a thousand questions of me, about my life, as if he's reconstructing every scene, I tell him everything, my mother, my father, childhood, my suspended dreams. We meet in the same place every time. Like a good-luck charm: Jor Bagh, Safdarjang's Tomb. I meet him here, park my car and we drive.

I never know where we're going, never ask, never want to know. He drives fast through the traffic, drives as if the other cars are not there, says this is the only way to do it, like you're in a video game, as if there's no one else in the world.

And in the car he watches me, has his eyes only half on the road.

One day I meet him at 8 a.m. and instead of driving we walk across to Lodhi Gardens in the pleasant morning heat. Feel the grass beneath our feet. Delhi has never been like this for me—I tell him so, I say I haven't known moments like these, this city is a prison with nowhere to go, but now this, so strange, a morning's walk, parakeets fluttering between the trees. *Ficus infectoria, Plumeria alba,* Latin names on signs. Along the rows of royal palm, on their bulbous bases, the carved graffiti of lovers' names. We stroll with the joggers, the walkers, the well-to-do and well-heeled, the retired army men of Def. Col., the judges and politicians of Lodhi Estate and Jor Bagh, the movers and shakers, the same ones who shop at Khan, the ones who have guards with rifles at their gates.

. . .

And sometimes after the grass on our feet, after Lodhi's regal ruins, below skies that are serene with cloud and touched by a tender breeze, we walk along to the Ambassador Hotel, inside to the Yellow Brick Road, for coffee and eggs at the breakfast buffet, for cornflakes and orange juice and toast, to sit in that bright sun-bleached room, poring over the menu and laughing at the words, pretending we're on holiday, seeing the pale tourists and starched businessmen passing through. It's a city transformed.

For three weeks it goes on like this. A quivering note sustained. He shows me this city, reveals it to me.

Back at home these days I can barely believe this is happening to me. When he drops me to my car at Jor Bagh and says good night I don't dare look in the mirror.

*

In the fire of Delhi we drive down Janpath, past the Imperial Hotel, on the way to Palika Bazaar in Connaught Place. He says he wants to show me something here, something I'd never find alone.

We leave the blasted light of the day behind to walk

the slope to the market underground, past the metal detectors that don't work, into the throng of subterranean bodies buying things. So I don't get lost he takes me by the hand and pulls me along. We navigate the shops, the people, the plastic, the video games, the men selling belts and hats and bags, the mountains of cheap bright junk that Delhi consumes. By the hand we steal through the crowd; he knows exactly where he's going: a faceless electronics store with an open front, small as a bathroom, identical to the rest.

In the shop he pushes through the crowd to reach a spiral metal staircase at the back and climbs straight up without pause.

The room above, this attic, has barely enough space for one to stand up straight, no windows, only bare bulbs, a fan blowing the stale hot air, and walls lined with cupboards containing thousands upon thousands of pirate DVDs. That's what he wants me to see, any film you need, anything you want. All the foreign films, going back a hundred years. The man who follows us up proudly says that all the foreigners come here, the embassy people, the film-makers too, actors, everyone, everyone comes to me. A black-market list of foreign films, Bergman, Kurosawa, Renais, Truffaut, Godard, the more obscure ones. They play a game with one another, he reels off a name and the man goes to a cupboard, picks out a stack, flips through it like a banker counting notes and hands over the correct plastic sleeve. He laughs, he can do this all day, he says.

They know each other well, he's a good customer, he's already devoured the list. Carnivorous in his tastes, he's bought and seen everything. He says he wanted to show me. He says, Choose whatever you want, pick as many as you like, it's my treat. The man slides open a cupboard and pulls out five piles. Shouts down the stairs for the boy to bring tea.

Out of the buried heat, at the stop lights on the edge of CP, pink-skinned tourists roam out of season on the pavements, on the short leash from the Imperial Hotel, ambushed by chess sets and peacock feathers and maps, swooped on by the hawkers and beggar girls. As we drive back south along Janpath, he motions over the wall to the Imperial, says, Do you know you can go into the hotel, leave your car with the valet, go in through the lobby, along the corridor, past the bathrooms, take a right at the bar, go outside along a pathway to the pool. At the pool you can give a fake name and room and you'll be handed a bottle of water, a towel and be left completely alone. A day by the pool, away from it all. It's possible. You just have to walk in as if you own the place, that's the trick; it's all about how you behave, and how you look, you have to go in with a certain disdain. It also helps if you wear shades.

I ask him about the PRESS sticker, the one on the back of the car—he says it's not real, he bought it in Karol Bagh, it's there to scare the cops, give them second thoughts at least, and also to open doors. A sticker and also a card. Any trouble and you wave it in their face, you buy some time with the right kind of talk. Another thing, he says, handing me his wallet. Open it. There, take out the top card on the right, the thick white one.

It reads: Deputy Commissioner of Police.

Do you know him?

No, he says, But I interviewed him once for a fake magazine, one I invented just for fun, to see what he'd say, to get hold of his card.

. . .

For three weeks it goes on. Three weeks like this, a glorious three. Giving the lie to the claim that time's a linear thing, a simple proposition from A to B. He says, You'll remember these days for the rest of your life. And though I laugh at him here, it's true. I will, I do. These three weeks that are amputated and cauterized, preserved in memory's specimen jar, lasting longer than the years before or since.

I still take refuge in their peaks. I watch the sun rise from them sometimes, sitting above the clouds before the avalanche of the present takes the ground from my feet. I'm still a girl here. My heart has not yet been broken in two. Everything has yet to happen, though it has already begun. He is still ugly, I am still beautiful. I am turned on. But if I stay here too long I get lost.

*

He tells me his story, talks to me about his exacting family, his schooldays, how he was a rebel with perfect grades, how his parents had schooled him beforehand, made him learn so many things, made him learn piano too, how the girls loved him for it, for his rebellion, his skill. How he could get away with murder if he wanted to.

He tells me about the girlfriends he had. About a girl he was with in school, how once she went away with her family on the train and he chased the train all night on a whim, drove after it in his car just to be at the station when she stepped off. Just to see the look on her face.

I ask him about the girls. Has he had many? With a casual smile he asks, Why do you want to know? And I say, Just because, that's all. So he tells me, Yes, he's had some. Enough to know. Would I like to know too?

We're driving down past AIIMS towards Green Park, towards the Outer Ring Road; we've been driving around for an hour. He looks at me, considers my silence.

I tell him I want to know, I want to know about them all, each and every one. What they were like, what they thought about the world, what he did with them.

Every time we meet we talk like this, pick it up and carry on. Each time I ask him and he tells me more. He willingly talks, describes their bodies to me, their lives, their pleasures and pains, the sex they had, how they fucked, the way their bodies combined. He watches my reaction to that word, and I stir, and every time we meet I ask for more.

*

We eat too, we measure life by our meals in the places he shows me, the canteen at the Andhra Bhavan, Basil & Thyme, Alkauser in Chanakyapuri. We eat in Connaught Place more than anywhere.

In the decaying chandelier ballroom of the United Coffee House, we have our own waiter here, we don't like to be served by anyone else. I tell myself that he knows something of us, that he's complicit somehow. This waiter of ours, his face is gaunt, high-cheekboned, with thick black hair, an Alexander nose, hard soul eyes. He's very handsome in a mountain way, Kashmiri, Himachali or Afghani, a killer, a nomad brought to earth, serving coffee and chicken à la Kiev. We decide he must be an actor in the end, one who is resting, or essaying a role, never just a waiter. His arrogance is peerless, matched only by his consummate professionalism, his excellence in the role, his simultaneous mastery and disdain for it. No one flicks a napkin like him, with such insouciant grace. He glides around the hall, never hurried or flustered. When it comes to your order he's almost disappointed by your choice, or else bored by the indecision when you can't pick your plate. A doubtful eye is placed somewhere else in the room, a hairline sneer appears. No matter how much you smile, he never smiles back, only nods. No matter how many times you thank him, however big a tip you leave, there's no reply. When he walks away we laugh. And yet he claims us every time, when we walk in he sees us and seats us.

In the restaurant we pore over the menu and gossip about the other diners, spy on them and make up their stories in this colonial relic, this memory of the Raj. We guess what people do, what they mean to one another, who's conducting an affair with whom, a century of secrets clinging to the stucco vaulted ceiling. Old genteel Delhi. A direct line to the British days, Ludlow Castle and Court Road. Before they bring in plasma TVs, before our waiter vanishes, never to be seen again.

*

We drive and we drive and he talks. He wants to show me every inch of the city, wants to exhaust me, fill my body with it, he wants me to know. To know the Ridge, the tail end of the Aravalli Hills stretching all the way from Gujarat, bursting up through the city like a dinosaur's back, one hundred and fifty million years old, older than the Himalaya itself, cutting across Delhi to die after the Hindu Rao Hospital and the Mutiny Memorial. To die without ceremony by the Yamuna.

Across boulders there are ghosts that haunt the Delhi Ridge. Across boulders, bodies of women have been draped rag-dollish, cut up, mutilated, their heads caved in with rocks, rotting to the earth, feeding the wild dogs. Bodies of men too, tumbled down in ruins of red, red rock. Across boulders, looming large, above and beyond, where the demons hide out in the scrub. We drive and we drive as the sun goes down, and here within the half-dead trees monkeys gather and men roam; they appear without warning at the side of the road, running out sometimes to flag you down.

. . .

It's the Southern Ridge he loves the best, he drives me there, around Tughlaqabad, the ruins of the ancient city, its desolate brawn of stone. He tells the legend of the Sufi saint, how he cursed the emperor who built these walls, condemned the fortress to be barren for evermore, populated only by animals and goatherds.

From the wild heart of Delhi this lonely city stands. Intruded and built upon, abandoned. There are forgotten monuments here, lost dreams. We've parked awhile by their side. Look, he says, watch the trees. Murders happen all the time, people vanish, men, women and children, in such a barren spot, the desolation of madmen, mystics, whores. A place as wild as anywhere in the world. Isn't it wonderful? He says he walks inside himself sometimes, there's nowhere else like it in the world.

Each day, as if our time is running out, we drive and talk. From Vasant Kunj to the farmhouses of Chhatarpur, through ancient Mehrauli.

Back again, overlooking Nehru Place. He stops to park at the side of the road, lights a cigarette. The scars of the twentieth century, the brutal Soviet blocks brushed in fine, choking dust, the crowds swarming in the gaps, charging the black market of computers, hardware, software. I'm worn down by him. He says, Look at what we've built. How wonderful it is to be alive.

Crepuscular. Delhi creeps as we go, the sun sinks behind the earth once more, bathes in the rotten Yamuna, drowns there. The temples erupt, the mosques, the droning of men's voices, the keening of every faith, the desperate plea for the sun to rise again, the bats and the birds, the great tambourine shake, a bedsheet shook over the balcony to the street. And the beasts of the Ridge are going wild, making a noise of pylons and wires, a cassette being rewound, unfurling tape against magnet, the madness of the dying sun, inducing ritual panic as old as the earth.

In a city such as this you still know the sun. You know the moment it appears, you hear the bells ringing madly in praise, hear the chanting and the call to prayer leaping into the sky, the wild dogs barking in the alleyways, rising from their beds of construction sand and dirt.

Driving to Vasant Vihar, where Baba Ganganath Road meets Nelson Mandela Marg, he stops the car at the high circle of rock that forms a roundabout there. Houses are built up there the way teeth grow from gums, hewn rock cemented on to ancient stone to make squat rooms painted in blue, pink, green, painted with advertising for soft drinks and petrol and butter. A cluster of families are living as if they've been shipwrecked, marooned. He says he goes and talks to them sometimes, spends hours sitting with them, telling them about the world, asking questions about their lives, making them laugh with his strangeness, with his wisdom, wandering in and out of them like a holy fool.

*

Further and further, more tangled in these lines, into the inferno night we go, into the reeling streets with the windows down, south past the pharmacies that leech on to AIIMS, past the families of patients waiting outside, past the narrow shopfronts and signboards of Green Park to the Qutb Minar, beyond the tombs and scrub into the desert, free of bodies and cars and rupee notes. Into the foundation emptiness of Gurgaon, to the construction sites that stretch monolithic, as far as the eye can see. He wants to show me the future. He wants to share the new world with me. We drive down these long, straight desert roads, built with nothing at their ends. They suddenly fall away around girders and steel poles. Construction appears, towering shells of concrete with sodium vapours illuminating the workers in the sky.

He gets off the road, turns the headlights out. Behind on the horizon Delhi is seething. And south, nothing but the vast nameless black of India exists. He says this is where the future lives. Apartment complexes, offices, townships, golf courses, malls, whole cityscapes not yet built, with names like Green Meadows and Marble Arch.

There's barely a sound out here. Only the distant echo of hammered metal. He lights a cigarette and touches my hand.

*

Holi. Here and now, as I write this. It's the end of winter, the beginning of spring. This morning the moon is the fullest it has been in eighteen years. The dogs are barking outside, going crazy. They've been barking since three in the morning without rest, echoing through the valley, in the courtyards, the front yards, the compounds, the jungle, the alleyways, the lanes.

Since three I've been awake.

I can feel my body being pulled skyward, or else the moon is about to fall on to me.

They play Holi in the morning, take the coloured powder and throw it about, smear it on your face. But I have nothing to do with that any more.

The Holi of my childhood, still laughing and running down the dry channels of the ditches, along the parched raised pathways between the fields, running with a paper windmill in my hand, colour scattered everywhere through the sky, laughing. But colour is used for revenge too, for spite and for power. For the lack of it. Under the cover of celebration a fistful of colour can smash against bone. Swarm upon a girl in an alleyway.

I'm remembering Holi in Delhi now. In the first year, a stubborn refusal to go outside as the men drink bhang and whip each other into a frenzy. The way trouble can start real fast. Semen dyed a dozen ways. All under the cover of colour. In the marketplace, hunting for prey, the spurned lover, the jilted heart. All under the cover of fun.

Holi just before him, Aunty is chastising me, cajoling me. Telling me I should be joining in, calling me difficult, saying it's tradition, it's who we are. But she's afraid of me too. She can't understand a person who doesn't want to belong to anything.

*

Descending into the city, driving at its heart. He takes me into Paharganj, that ink blot on the consciousness of Delhi, the spot on the map obscuring it black. One of those places good Delhiites don't go, a ghetto of back-packer foreigners and dirty liars, con men, beggars, cheats, a place of drugs, a place of adventure, a Disneyland of white skin, vacancy taped across the eyes, foreigners like film-set refugees waiting to be airlifted, and those who make a living of them, of their need and their fear, waiting for the new arrivals, picking out the weak from the strong.

. . .

This place in April, the touts and crooks, the toilet paper on sale. Israelis, Japanese, Germans, English, not many Americans, one or two with tousled, floppy hair and chinos, clutching guidebooks. And the Japanese boy whose face is on the wall of every guest house and café— missing eight months, last seen in Manali, presumed dead.

He knew this place well; he guided me through the alleys with ease. He took me to see a friend of his who is frozen in my mind even now. Franklin John.

Perhaps it's because of the photograph. We had a camera with us that day, he carried his Pentax and took a picture of Franklin and it came out all blurred on black-and-white film, but somehow that suited him, it matched his face. Taken in the smeared room in the backstreets, junked to his eyeballs, full of grace. The patron saint of Paharganj.

*

We are walking away from the main bazaar, he knows where he's going, he cuts in and out of the alleyways until he reaches a guest house full of travellers, climbs the stairs inside and raps on a door.

In the photograph of Franklin his face is obscured, his body too, though its outline says enough. It holds the spectre of his muscles, their graphitic blur. Though wasted away, they are still enough to kill a man.

He was in motion the moment the photo was shot, talking at us until the needle hit the vein. He moved around the room in anticipation of it the way a boxer moves around the ring, his mouth the jab, the needle the knockout punch. In his fifties, a body of hardship and experience, an Irishman from Galway, with a history of junk as long as his arm. His hair is cropped close to his head, a Caesar cut for a backstreet emperor. His eyes are blue. They fix on you, they don't shy away. He could be dead now too, I'll never know.

I see him frozen in this photo and then I see him in the flesh with the needle in his hand full of the heroin he's bought from the Kashmiris downstairs. It's shit, he says.

He talks about the good stuff, the opium in Pushkar, the junk in Amritsar. He knows India in a way I never will, a country that doesn't exist for me. There's the malarial buzz in the corridor, the underwater echo of sounds, the drone of fans, the faint strumming of guitars in other rooms. Check the door is locked shut. I watch him hold the lighter to the spoon, his bare feet collecting dust. There is so much care to his preparation, it's just like puja.

He finds the vein, presses the syringe into his skin, his eyes glaze over into glorious death. Then he's crouched in the cold shower, naked aside from his underwear, I see him through the open door. Afterwards he crawls, pulls some trousers on, drags himself under the bed and bends into a ball, mumbling to himself for an hour like an old man. There are four other people in the room, two Israelis, a Dane and an Englishman, all stoned out of their minds, just back from a trip to the mountains. I'm introduced as a friend but they don't care. They'll forgive anything, they don't know what's going on. They pass the chillum around invoking Shiva. He takes it and inhales harder than everyone.

*

He asked about Aunty all the time, about my mother and father, even Uncle. He was fascinated by them all, he wanted to get to the heart of them. He listened, rapt at my reports of the dinner table, at my memories of childhood, he laughed at their ideas, nodded lovingly at my life. He said everyone was afraid, because they couldn't see any more. But you don't owe them anything. Why do you cling so hard?

*

Then one day, instead of driving, he asks if I'd like to see his apartment. He says the renovations are almost done, that it only needs painting and he can unpack and settle in. Would I like to see it? I say I would.

His apartment is like no place I've seen. Cut off from Delhi, cut off from the earth, turned into a kind of maze, then sealed. Terracotta and black granite floors. There are empty spaces cut into the inside walls, they look out into the central hallway so fragments of every room can be viewed, so nothing is private inside.

. . .

He says he designed it himself. As if it were a bunker at the end of the world.

He walks me around: bedroom, hallway, kitchen, living room, balcony, one looking into the next. It's only in the bathroom at the rear where the original home remains untouched, old, charming, possessed by the clank of pipes, with the big pale light that streams through the frosted glass. In here you can feel the heat and light of Delhi.

We sit out on his balcony for an hour in the morning sun, among the boxes of his life that are waiting to be unpacked. The balcony is surrounded by a high bamboo fence with creeping plants all around, so you can only see the sky. Without friends, without family, without servants. He says you can walk around naked if you want, no one would ever know.

*

A few days later we're driving from CP around India Gate. I am holding an empty Coke can between my legs.

He looks at it and says, Can I get that for you? Can I throw it away? And I say, No, it's OK. I like something between my legs.

Pointedly. A calculated phrase. He looks at me.
   This is all it takes.

*

All the marriage meetings I ever had ended in the same rejection. What they never understood was that I had rejected them long before they saw my face.

The first boy was from a middle-class family much like my own. He had a steady job as an engineer. Aspirational, shining with belief, with the ambition to go to the States himself. He had learned his role by rote. We met in the Defence Colony Barista in the March of my first Delhi year. I had no car then. Aunty escorted me, waiting in the back seat like a pimp while her driver ate chaat in the market outside. She made me wear a kurta and jeans, to be both modern and traditional at once.

. . .

He was already waiting for me inside. He had his laptop open at the low table. I recognized him from the photo in the résumé that had been sent, that had just been thrust beneath my nose, and he looked up and recognized me in turn. Aunty had sent a photograph of me, taken at a studio set up at one of the wedding functions we'd attended. In a sari, a little tipsy, in the glare of the artificial light, with a posed, enforced smile, the photo stripped me of my life.

I remember very clearly the pen he kept in the top pocket of his shirt, also the new glasses he wore. They were designer, he proudly said. But his face I don't recall, his was like the million others I saw. He was simply his glasses and his pen and the starched white shirt. He talked to me from the start about the importance of family, about his mother, what his mother thought about things. My mother says, he said many times, and he listed what they looked for in a girl. I sat across from him silent, sullen, angry with myself because I had agreed to be there at all. He said he wanted a girl who was simple, respectful, but educated of course, able to have her own opinions. But she must be respectful to his mother above all else. They must get on or there'd be no point. I felt quite sick at the mechanics of it. But Aunty had told me again and again, Marriage is not about love, when will you understand this? Love is a luxury that doesn't exist in the real world.

I asked him drily if it wouldn't be better for me to meet his mother alone. Without a flicker of understanding he said no.

When it came it was one of those polite rejections, where his mother tells Aunty that he's found someone else absolutely perfect that very same day, what timing, what coincidence. What to do? Aunty smiles. What to do. But she's kicking herself. What did you say? You don't know how to talk to people, to show yourself in the best light, you don't stand up straight, you don't smile.

The next boy was from a south Delhi business family, the only son and heir, twenty-six years old. We met in another coffee shop, all around us you could spy these marriage meetings taking place. This boy was more arrogant, wealthy, dressed in a designer shirt, he wore his fat with pride, was well groomed, his pouting lips protruding from his face, his eyes heavy lidded, stirring his tea very slow. Well-manicured fingers perched on the table like exotic birds. There was something in his manner that spoke of cruelty to me. He talked at length, about his Hyundai, his plan to replace it with a Mercedes before the year was out. And all the while he eyed me with a measure of disdain. Why he ever agreed to meet me in the first place I'll never know. But Aunty was punching above her weight, saying, Nothing succeeds like success.

*

We make love on the first of May, Labour Day. A day for the workers.

His apartment is being painted, it's full of them but he sends them home, tries to explain the concept of it as he does, this day to honour the working people of the world, but it's lost on them completely, everything about it is lost. They down tools and go anyway.

He says, Go home, get drunk, make love to your wives. They look at me as they go.

. . .

He'd waited until they arrived to tell them they were free, until they'd begun to work, to make it worthwhile, to see their reaction. Because theatre was important. But we'd planned this. I'd told him I wanted to know what it was like, I was ready, I wanted it to be him.

*

We've been drinking since the workers left. Drinking to remove the awkwardness in me.

Most of the other rooms have been finished, already painted in purple, black, red or ink blue. But in the bedroom the walls are still white.

Everything smells of paint in here. The smell catches in my nostrils, the back of my throat. The AC is on high. Outside it's approaching forty degrees. Beating the earth.

In the kitchen the fridge is well stocked: water, juice, soft drinks, a crate of beer. Several bottles of good whisky in the cupboard. There are cold cuts in the fridge, from the charcuterie in Vasant Vihar, bresaola, serrano, chorizo. He teaches me how to say these words, how to say "charcuterie," from the French, obsolete: *char* for flesh, *cuite* for cooked, cooked flesh, flesh that is cooked, which we eat.

He pours a glass of whisky for me, Caol Ila. Teaches me to say that too, tapping the tip of the tongue to the roof of the mouth, mixing it with some drops of clean water, saying, This is the way. In the dhabas the whisky's dirty, you drink it with Coke, with soda, but not this. He rolls it around the glass. It coats the side and falls, like amber for fossils. Smell it, he says, close your eyes. And he raises the glass to my nose. It smells of earth and sea and salt, Bombay without the heat, in the glint of stars and mud and leaves, in woodsmoke sluiced through rain. Now taste it. I take the glass from his hands, bring it up to my lips. It burns as it touches them. He kisses it back from me and delicately, with his hands on my hips, presses himself against me. I feel the hardness of him. I bring the glass up, fill my mouth, kiss him back again. He looks up, almost surprised, like a boy.

. . .

Now wait. In the empty bedroom he smokes a cigarette, and I make up the bare mattress with a fresh white sheet. Wait. Now I'm standing before him taking off my clothes, covering myself with my arms.

Wait. He's lowering me down, I'm breathing him in as he's looming over me with his enormous eyes, like the statue of a dictator waiting to fall.

When it happens it hurts.

And then it doesn't hurt. Pain slips away into the distance of a blizzard, and beyond all that, with eyes closed, chest cracked open, ribcage pulled apart, my heart fills up with the driving snow.

I didn't know what to do afterwards. I lay there still as a corpse in the mortuary sheets, a vacancy of limbs, not daring to move in case it marked an end, but he was a part of me, his ugliness, his black skin. I held it all. Falling in and out of sleep with a pin drop of pain somewhere else.

. . .

He's in the bathroom now. He's come back with a cigarette. He's lying next to me. He's hard again. He puts the
cigarette to my lips, holds my gaze, opens my legs, with
his hand he guides himself in.

*

Seeming to wake from nowhere suddenly from the cold,
I ask for a blanket. Instead he switches off the AC.

Little by little Delhi encroaches. You can hear it. You can
see the thin sliver of sunlight on the frame of the window, fading to dusk. Slowly you make out the noise of
children laughing and playing in the lane behind, pans
being washed there and traffic beyond.

The bathroom has retained the day's heat. The air is so
thick in here you can swim in it. In the shower we stand
and he washes me, his body behind mine, his hand on my
belly where my heart beats, he brings it down, puts one
hand around my neck, one inside. I move away, I sit at
the side to watch him. There's muscle around his bones,

not a shred of fat on him, and there are scars across his back that I see. We go back into the room to sleep.

When I wake again it is night, the room has been filled with it, the headlights of cars shift along the fabric of the curtain, rise up the wall and are gone. The whisky bottle is half-empty. He's not here with me.

I find him in the dark of the balcony, crouching naked, one hand against the bamboo, his head tilted, listening. He turns towards me, puts his finger to his lips.

Shhh, he says. Listen.

In the dargah of Nizamuddin the qawwalis are playing. He says, Do you hear them? Let's go before it's too late.

*

His same sense of theatre demands we wear the right clothes. He unlocks a cupboard inside, tells me to look through it, pick out something to wear. It's full of discarded items, from family, cousins, his mother, old girl-friends maybe. His parents lived here before, left many things behind. I find a salwar-kameez, he takes out a long white kurta for himself from his own wardrobe, and in it he becomes dignified, sober, seeming older. And me, I watch myself in the mirror, covering my head with the dupatta, wrapping it around my forehead, behind my ears, around my neck, to frame my face, and I become Persian, dark-eyed, pious, transformed.

We laugh in the mirror and he holds me, touches my face, tucks my hair away.

He sits to crumble charas into a mixing bowl. I watch in fascination. Do you want to try? You'll like it, he says. He says it comes from the mountains, a deep rich scent from Parvati Valley, he'll take me there one day. Here, smell it. He holds it to my nose. Then I watch as he heats it, crumbles it in the bowl, burns the cigarette, adds the tobacco, mixes it reverently, rolls. Lights it, praises Shiva, takes a long drag and hands it over to me. He says to take it all the way in, down to the base of the lungs, hold it there as long as I can.

*

We left the apartment that night and walked along the streets, walking without touching. Through Nizamuddin in the heat to the dargah, from the smart, clipped neighbourhood into the Muslim streets, where bearded men gathered in white and goats were tethered to butchers' shops. Left at the mosque, down the passageway, the night brighter than the day, eerie in its calligraphic pharmacy, in Urdu glowing green and gold, trimmed by the desert and the certainty of God. Men stood in their shops behind counters, beside TVs showing preachers delivering sermons, voices droning out of loudspeakers, the flutter of rose petals, a butcher's knife.

The crowds were swirling in the narrowing alleyway, the walls closing in at the sides, canopied with cloth, drawing us down lower, almost underground, as if we were being sucked downriver to a grotto. So many bodies there that we were almost lost. He grabbed my hand to keep me close. The threshold of the dargah appeared, medieval. We crossed over.

. . .

It is said that the dargah is not only a place on earth, it is also a rupture in space and time, a portal through which the saint can enter this world.

We remove the chappals from our feet, add them to the rising pile. Bump against the mass of bodies, step on the black-and-white marble that like a riverbed has been worn down, smoothed by centuries of pilgrims' feet, its corners like melted wax. Red petals fleck the ground, fluttering on to graves.

Inside, the river of people dissipates; it finds new currents, reaches up into the sky. Pilgrims slow down, scatter, form groups, they find corners for themselves, as if striking camp.

The eight players of the qawwali are sitting in the inner courtyard before the shrine, sitting in two banks of four, lining one side of a rectangle. Devotees and onlookers form the two long edges, thirty or forty of them now, their numbers increasing all the time. Everyone faces inwards to the centre they have made, a void and a well in the middle of the bodies in which the song is amplified. It has been going for an hour now.

The tabla and dholak inducing a trance.

The harmonium guiding the leader's voice.

Handclaps locking the rhythm inside.

The leader is gnomic, bold and erect, his beard hangs down his chest in a point, his eyes crinkle above it in a smile. And his voice, it undulates within the scaffold of his throat, rising to a pure note with his hand held high.

Hypnotized, forgetting ourselves, we take a place at the back of one side, enclosed in the heat, standing at the back of the crowd. We crane our necks to see. At the front they are seated, swaying, hijras among them, their painted eyes rolling around their heads.

In space, beyond the sun and moon, in the depthless universe where the stars can't be seen, there is the saint.

The music grows faster, wilder, careening towards rupture, the crowd grows so that we are pressed against one another by those around, but I can feel him, feel his body next to mine, his hand around my own. As the rhythm builds we are pushed forward until we emerge somehow at the front of the standing group. Here we remain poised on the edge.

We begin to forget ourselves, who we are, our daily lives, for half an hour we remain like this.

Then the miracle happens.

The leader in full song looks up at me, looks me in the eyes, and in the middle of his plaintive cry motions with his hand for us to sit at the front of the crowd.

The crowd parted, it did, the people smiled and moved aside, hands steadied our path, faces beamed at us, bodies rocked themselves possessed.

And now sat at the front on my heels, fists on knees in the desert heat with the hot wind of Delhi that scours our skin, with faces etched in the rhythm and bound in the love of the saint, my entire being a percussive beat, and even he who has given me this is gone.

I am disappeared. On a plateau of rock, burst into flames.

I fall into a trance. I lose myself. How long I remain like this I can't say, but it feels like hours have passed when I open my eyes. People are looking and smiling. For as long as the music plays the world is mine.

But it wears down, it eases off, exhaustion follows, and the leader seems to avert his gaze.

Without the beat to hold us in place our hearts release themselves like birds up into the night sky. We begin to drift. Electric light falls on the land.

And walking home through the city, listening to its womb-sound, we are conquerors. We don't say another word. Hungry, bereft, slipping through the alleyways, it's only when we get back to his home that the desire returns. It comes with the force of everything we've heard. We do it again right there against the door, without undressing. He lifts me up and holds me against the wall. With sanctity, grief and passion, I bite into his flesh and he puts himself inside me and he bursts.

Aunty thinks I'm sleeping at a classmate's house. When I call her to say good night he takes the phone from me and he speaks as my friend's imaginary father, in an assured voice that is casual, measured, having just the right tone. He's such a convincing liar.

*

It goes on all night, until disintegration. He drinks his whisky and worships me, and I give my body to him, feed my skin, take his black lips and hold them to the childish fat around my waist, the heat between my legs. I let him come to me. With such abandon, such a lack of care. And such terror on seeing the daylight appear through the cracks, to find the room becoming visible again, to know dull shapes are real things once more. Lying down at the end of it, upheld in the empty thoughts of what we've done. I'd forgotten the night would ever end.

*

I woke around eleven. In those few moments of unre-membering, of pure animal consciousness unattached to the world, I saw him beside me, felt the pain in my hips, the tearing in me, and the dull tobacco warmth of his breath.

He stirred and rolled closer, opened his eyes, and for the briefest moment his face was ungoverned, appearing monstrous. But his pupils dilated, turned cunning, and when he blinked he hid the animal away. Good morn-ing, he said. He reached to light a cigarette and smiled.

We did it again, painfully this time, all too real. Every nerve tapped and twisted, with nothing to numb it, I cried out, lost in the fields, and I held him as he poured himself into me. Like the pressing of a bruise, the plea-sure of pain, I love him for this.

He held me in his arms afterwards, held me round my waist, pressed his teeth to the back of my neck, whis-pered in my ear, and he asked me what it was I wanted from the world, what it was I feared. I said I feared everything, and I only wanted to be free.

.   .   .

Later I showered, brushed my teeth and got changed. While he made breakfast he coached me on what to say to Aunty. Already we have slipped into a pattern, there are things we don't mention any more, movements that are unquestioned, the shorthand of lovers, things that are understood.

I drive home as if in slow motion, floating above the noise as the city parts for me. It's such a sudden switch inside where Aunty is dressed in a fine sari, preparing to go for a kitty party, putting on earrings in the strip-light mirror, filling an envelope with money and chatting away, trying to make me get changed to go along with her, but there's no time, she's already running late. She leaves me alone.

In the silence left behind, inside my room, I close my eyes. In the bathroom I take a shower and revel in the water's heat. I examine my body closely, look for marks and wondrous signs. Then, with the ghost of his cock between my legs and Aunty far away, I fall into a deep and turbulent sleep.

TWO

Now I'm remembering the day a year later when I heard that he'd died. He was dead three weeks already then, already cremated, his ashes scattered by his parents in the Ganga at Rishikesh. That's right, his parents, alive and well and in the flesh.

I was sitting next to Aunty on the sofa when the call came in. His driver, Ali, was on the line. He had a driver by that point, he'd found him in a slum colony drinking one night and they'd hit it off, he'd given him the job on a whim. Ali loved him like they all loved him, all his men. Now sobbing, drunk, half out of his mind, he gathered himself enough to say, Madam, no one has told you, but I have to tell you, it's my duty . . . Sir is no more, he is dead.

I listened to his sobbing and I hung up without a word, and as we continued to watch the TV a white-hot surge shot from my temples through my skin.

Still I didn't believe it was true, not at first. In the moment of shock I told myself it was a game, that after months of silence it was the beginning of his revenge. Throughout the night I went over all the things that had gone between us, how it had come to this, and I met the dawn staring at the vacant window in the tower block across the way. Then, with barely any sleep, I resolved to drive to his apartment to confront him and finish this once and for all.

July 3rd. It was raining that day. The monsoon hung over the city in a tepid kind of grey, not with the driving force that exhilarates but the squalid sort that seeps into your bones. I hadn't been near Nizamuddin since I'd seen him the final time, and when I turned into the colony all the memories came rushing back at me, banging on the windows like beggar girls. Still I rehearsed my lines, I prepared a defiant speech.

But when I pulled up across the road I knew there was no need. The bamboo wall of the balcony had been torn down, the front door and the windows were all wide open and an ugly white light shone on a handful of well-dressed people within.

As I entered they were standing in the living room, engaged in sober conversation. The room had been stripped clean and there were packing crates along one wall. I don't know what I said at that moment, but I must have looked disturbed to them, exhausted, con-fused and soaked by the rain. The entire group seemed to back away, all except three: a couple in their sixties, elegant but severe, and a hard-edged girl several years older than I.

It was the girl who spoke first. In a tired voice she said, Who are you? and when I found I couldn't answer she nodded as if she knew the answer anyway. Then I asked the question back of them, Who are you? Who are they? To which she replied that they were his parents and she was his fiancée, and he was dead now, so it would be better for everyone if I just turned around and went away.

We don't drive around Delhi any more, we stay in his apartment and we fuck. And also we make love. He is a god to me. I've never known with such certainty what my body is for.

I've told Aunty I'm enrolled in a summer language course. I say I'm learning French. That it will aid my studies, my future career, my marriage prospects. It will help to take me abroad one day. This is his idea of course, he tells me to say these words. He says she'll accept them, that they'll work. And it's true—despite an initial protest, she's pleased.

. . .

Inside the apartment the renovation is complete. His belongings are moved back into place, the paint is dry, the AC runs day and night.

Up the white marble stairs, we enter through the heavy wooden door, across the dark hallway, to the living room that's partitioned by Japanese sliding screens.

There's a vast TV in there, an expensive stereo, low sofas, cushions, Afghan rugs, piles of books and magazines on the coffee table, standing lamps with warm bulbs and art prints on the wall. There's a writing desk, too, with his computer on it, a still-empty bookshelf, and the high bamboo-walled balcony beyond the black glass doors.

In his bedroom the walls are painted red, with one small window to let faint light in. It's bare save for the bed that sprawls across the terracotta floor. A scaffold of inter-locking tubes, he says there's only one way of putting it together and taking it apart.

. . .

This bedroom, this red floor, that black bed, those white sheets. That long space like a fish tank cut into the inside wall, to look out on the corridor, for invisible faces to observe.

In a niche above the bed he has a shrine to Shiva. Nataraj, the dancing Lord, who stands in a dark hole with a small warm bulb giving fire from behind, summoning the chaos of the world.

There's a recess in the bedroom too, big enough for a body to fit. He places me inside there, asks me to pose for him. He photographs me here. Like a statue he watches me, admires my body, my face, adores my youth. In the recess, in profile, my knees pulled up to my bare chest, arms clasped around them, spine curved, hair tied up on the top of my head, carved out in silhouette. I hold my breath. Sitting naked, cross-legged, he photographs me. On hands and knees, not moving, he tells me to stay and takes my image and watches me. Then he paces the room, cigarette in hand, like a critic, examining me from all angles before he goes to get a beer, goes to the kitchen to make some food, to the living room to watch TV. Tells me not to move, until I think I've been forgotten. Then he comes back in, opens my legs.

He says there should be two of me. One forever in that place and one for the world. He'd fuck one on the bed and watch the other up there.

Other times he just wants to lie inside. He comes up and enters, wraps his arms around me, holds me from behind, says he'd frame me if he could, pin me like a butterfly to the page. He holds my head in a certain light, positions me by the chin. My arms, my neck, my nose, my heart—so perfect a set of things they could break.

I find to my surprise that I don't mind hearing these words, that I like him doing these things to me. I find I'm happy to make an object of myself for him, he who is setting me free.

*

It's getting light at 5 a.m., the heat has never left. It's so hot these days that the tarmac melts and no one really sleeps. I wake and I drive into the city. I arrive at his apartment and let myself in. I find him asleep, in bed or in the living room. I press myself into him. The apartment is unmoving. No one is ringing the doorbell, there's no sound of soap operas on TV, no servants sweeping around our feet. There's only this.

The vendors wheel their carts along the road. Above his balcony the black kites circle, looking like sharks seen from the ocean floor. His head is between my legs, his gleaming mouth gnawing at my flesh. Day ends and night falls again and again, and each night I have to go home. With my black hair shining I shower and get dressed and I go.

At home I talk about my course, I bore Aunty with it, I even speak some small phrases of French he has taught me. I tell her little anecdotes about the people there, the friends I've made, the ones I hate. I talk about the friends' houses that I have begun to study in, talk about their parents who don't exist. Lies on top of lies, as easy as breathing. People and lives constructed out of nothingness. I keep her happy with gossip, make her intimate with it. It's still necessary, even at twenty, to do these things.

But when I'm with him there is only the truth of his apartment, his car and the city in which we move. I see his eye on me above all things. In his living room, with the lights off, in the glow of the TV, watching movies: *Pickpocket, Hiroshima Mon Amour, La Jetée, Night of the Living Dead.* He fixes his eye, follows my face for every twitch, each smile, each moment of delight and surprise, sadness and pain, he says he's never seen a face like mine, he could watch it all day. All those years of eyes on me, all that fear, and it has come to this, this desire that is in me alone.

Lying on my back. He comes into me. His eyes flutter behind their lids. I say, I knew you were watching me in the café. I knew it long before. I was sitting there for a long time. I could feel your eyes on me. I smile at the memory, say to myself, Your beautiful face. I pull him close, reach round to feel the scars on his back, ask where they came from. He barely acknowledges the question, his breath is shortening in concentration, he's losing the power of speech, slowly rising, slowly falling into me. With his eyes closed he finds the breath for it, tells me they're very old, from his childhood, they grew up with him.

There are long moments when nothing exists. She lies on her back. Their heads are touching, their bodies drifting apart in a V. They look at one another. The AC fights against the oven outside. They catch their breath awhile.

Smiles fade and the thoughts remain. She says, Let me see them again. He rolls to his side and she examines his scars in the cathedral light. He's not ashamed. She's fascinated by their texture, by their memory of pain. She places her fingers upon them. This is inevitable. It's inevitable too that she brings her mouth close, kisses them, touches them with her tongue, moves her tongue along their ridges. He opens his eyes to this, she can feel it happening, she can hear him holding his breath. She says, Does it hurt? and he turns to her, cups her face in his hands.

. . .

Out on the street nothing stirs. It's too hot for anything now. The city is disappearing from view. We lie in bed and we barely move, we hide from the bleached white weight of the sun that throbs like a migraine on the land. In this darkened room I hold his cock in my hand, and for hours we are like this in half-sleep.

Then night is here. The wailing of the dargah begins. The tree-tangled temples glow with their flags and their bells inside. Sounds change in the dark, some imperceptible quality of the air alters them, a quality of thickness, permeability, as if the sun has been an infinite wall and the darkness an absence that amplifies. Voices clamour from the pavement. Trains come and go from Nizamuddin station. I hear the longing in their departure. I've started to smoke his joints with him, see their curls that are lit by the headlights of cars. I listen to the horns on Mathura Road.

Lodhi Road joining Mathura Road. The curious witchcraft of junctions. The ruins of Neeli Chhatri in the middle of the traffic circle, connecting us. We walk around it. We talk through our story all the time. We talk through our story and make a myth of it, let it solidify, see it cool in the bed. Over and over I ask him, What did you see that day? What were you doing in the café? We celebrate ourselves this way. I like to hear it when it comes from his lips. He says, I saw a blank slate, a lump of wet clay.

With me, like this, he's the happiest he's been. I give it to him, I raise him up. He pulls me down, puts his lips to my hole. The balance of this goes on for hours. For hours I'm consumed, and when I leave he remains a mountain in his shadow room.

*

But very early on he gives me a sign of how it will end, if I'm wise. We're sitting on the sofa in his living room, looking at the empty bookshelf against the wall. Looking at the boxes full of books by its side. New ones, old ones. He's been to Fact and Fiction in Vasant Vihar, bought a hundred books; he's hauled two hundred more from New York. The day is white-hot outside. We're naked, and I've told him that a bookshelf without books is a terrible thing. So he says, Fill it up, go ahead, the job is yours.

It takes the whole morning. A perilous operation. One false move and the spell is broken. Naked he sits on the sofa with an icebox of beer by his side, and naked I stalk the room. He watches me crouching and opening the boxes, placing the books on the floor, and he drinks as I run my fingers along their spines.

I stop at a book now and then, leaf through its pages. Sit down and read before deciding where to place it. I debate how to arrange them, whether they should be done alphabetically, by size, by style, or some clever combination of it all. I take pleasure in whispering these questions to myself. He says, You whisper to yourself all the time. I never noticed it before. He wants to know what I say, I say it's nothing, just words. Reassurances for myself.

Every now and then I go to take a sip of his beer. Sometimes I take a book of photography and sit with him, and we look through the images together then, I spend hours like this, with Araki, Prabuddha, Moriyama and Klein. With black-and-white photos of naked women he's culled from magazines, Kate Moss and tribeswomen and Japanese girls bound in rope.

When I find a passage of text that I like I read it out to him. He never interrupts. He listens to me, tells me to speak and we get lost in it, in my own voice and in his listening to me. There are goosebumps on my arms and legs, the soft hairs stand on end. I come over to the sofa and climb into his lap, continue to read, watch his hands sliding over the tautness of my skin, dipping in. And all the time he continues to drink.

Then it happens that I forget him entirely. The performance stops and my work goes on. For an hour or more I lose myself so completely in the task and I'm the same girl I've ever been, the tongue poking out of the corner of my mouth, the same as I was when I was six years old, pensive, curious, not fit for the world.

When it's over I stand back to admire my handiwork. And proud, calling out to him, turning around, I discover he's passed out from the beer, twelve in total, one after the other without pause. And unable to keep control or wake, he's pissed himself; there's a wide dark patch on the sofa dripping to the floor between his legs.

Like my grandfather he is a godman. Like him, he has things to say. He speaks of Shiva to me, and I have become his disciple on the dusty road. Convincing, persuading, cajoling me. He gives his sermon as he speaks, of another future, of revolution in the villages, in the towns and cities, the revolution of technology, the Internet, new connections and networks. Revolution in India, this is how it will be: no war, no guns, only technology, this he truly believes. He tells me how these connections will occur, how the poor will see and hear, how there will be empowerment for all, how Shiva guides him, and of this world he will be the king.

Like my grandfather, who spoke in tongues. Who had the light of God in him, barefoot from town to dusty town. Who roamed the lands that are the future now, the townships and malls and garbage dumps.

. . .

He worked in a bank when he lived in the world, a shy, nervous man. He worked quietly there for years behind the metal grille, behind the screens in the back room, counting money, making copies of copies of forms by the crumbling yellow walls. And then every so often he would get up and start to walk.

Straight out of the door, across the fields to the horizon. He'd walk for days sometimes and sometimes weeks, give all his possessions away. Lose his clothes, find new ones, wear rags, not shave, grow his hair and his beard, get that desert look in his eyes. They'd find him beneath a banyan tree in a far town, holding forth with a crowd, giving sermons, reciting the Gita and the Upanishads by heart. From where he learned them no one knew. They seemed to have been carved on his heart with a blade.

At the start they went out to find him, to bring him back like a wayward teen. But every time he walked right out again. Soon enough they grew to indulge him, to leave him alone, they stopped searching, they washed their hands of him, they cursed him and sighed and said, Let it be his fate. He'd always wander back in the end, walk in through the door one day. Like everything, it was just allowed to go on. The bank kept his job for him. He'd go back there every time, turn up for work and no one would say anything, though it's hard to believe. So there were two men in him, one hidden at home and one forever wandering the plains.

*

But it's the history of women that's the history of migration. Men hold the line and they remain. They go to war, they go for work, they travel the land, but they remain. Their name remains, their land remains. You can follow their line into the dark. How to trace the line of women, how to find from where we came? Every generation stripped away. Passed to another name. Gone the line and the name. They never belonged to us anyway. The earth doesn't belong to us. We disappear, we do not remain.

*

When I left his apartment the day I learned of his death, Ali was alone a short distance away on the road, despondent, full of grief, his body hanging limp in the rain with his long fingers around his thighs as if he were preparing to be sick. I was halfway to my car before he saw me there and it was only then that he came to life, running after me and calling out, shouting, Madam, madam, please stop.

Ali is standing outside my car door, I can see him. He's on the street, knocking on the window, trying the handle, saying something that I cannot hear. The rain has become heavier, bouncing off the front of the car, and his face is covered in tears, his eyes are red with crying and drink. He is begging me to please open up, to speak to him, to wind down the glass and open the door so he can speak to me, Please, madam, please. He is drenched, rain has dishevelled his hair, rain is dripping from the beak of his nose. And he is snivelling in a way that I cannot bear. He begs, he starts to slap the glass, struggles with the handle, his face is twisting out of shape. People on their balconies are watching. Guards are stepping out into the street. They know what this is about. From the balcony the fiancée is shouting, ordering Ali away. I can't take it. Can't look at him. I start the engine and drive.

.   .   .

I drive for hours. Numb, my whole body shivering, teeth chattering, an ashen face looking at itself in the mirror when it dares. I try to think of a place I can go, somewhere or someone to whom I can turn, a street where I can park without memory, some quiet colony where I can clear my head. But there is nothing, nowhere. Every time I stop, accusing faces look in at me. Maids and servants walking by, housewives and aunties, guards telling me to move. Through the blur of rain I can barely see the road.

At some point a calm descends. It comes at the limit of exhaustion, from something being extinguished. I turn the car around and I begin to drive home. On the way I stop one last time by the Purana Qila. I pull to the side here, take out the SIM card from my phone, bend it in two and throw it in the road.

*

We wait for the monsoon to break. The black clouds are gathering over Humayun's Tomb, the kites ride the thermals above its domes. We run our hands over the sandstone walls, walk the boundaries of Nizamuddin.

The morning is already swollen, in the middle of the day it dims, it might as well be dawn again the way the light drops out and the clouds roll in, cities themselves, blotting the sun.

Then the first big drops of rain descend. Plop, plop, plop. Bombs of rain one day, big as insects, splashing up the choking red dust, sending it into the atmosphere, trowelling nostrils in the thick cake of earth, and in the smell of wet tarmac rising up we rejoice. People have come out to stand in the streets, on to their balconies to soak themselves in it. We lie on his balcony as it turns to a deluge, as the drops grow together and the thunder cuts the air.

*

Rain pours down, the city floods. Thunder and lightning fill the sky. And the junctions, they've become waterlogged, silt has clogged the drains that are never cleaned. I still go on visits with Aunty here, in a car with water up to the axles in places, stuck in traffic, carrying gifts. I still sit with her at dinner, see Uncle trotting in and out of his room, still answer her questions, listen to her prattle on about the NRI. All this life goes on. But I don't remember a thing of it.

I remember him instead. He's following me in the street. The rain-slicked pathways, potholes as puddles, the pools created in the roads, sunlight breaking through the cloud sculpting deep shadows, bringing colour and heat and bouncing light from the sheets. In the evening the head-lights graze upon black umbrellas open at crossroads, disembodied toes avoiding the splash of cars and autos. Auto drivers queued up outside Khan. We play games like this: I message him, tell him which market or colony I'll visit, where I plan to shop, South Extension, GK I, Sarojini Nagar. And he will be there, hidden among the crowds, searching to find me there. I'll catch a glimpse of him from the corner of my eye. Sometimes I'll never see him at all. I'll walk from shop to shop, conscious of my straightened back, my breasts, the arch of my neck. I'll go back home and undress as he tells me where I've been.

Then I arrive at his apartment one day and there are clothes laid out for me on the bed. Clothes he has bought, which he wants me to wear. He says they'll suit me, that it's time to become someone new.

He watches as I examine them, measuring my response. They are cool clothes, clothes from the parties in Goa, clothes from the raves: tight T-shirts, cargo pants, a psychedelic T-shirt of Shiva, another with Ganesh. Fluorescent colours. He says, Try them, put them on, and the authority in his voice that is always so absolute is cut with something else. I do it for him without complaint. I undress, I take off my jeans and T-shirt, stand in front of him naked and put them on.

He watches while I dress, and as I do so he holds his breath, getting hard, and when it's done he comes towards me, puts his hands on me.

In Delhi it was the time of the Cyber Mehfil. A small window of belief, an explosion of parties and raves at the turn of the century, voices celebrating the new millennium, the opportunities it held, the freedom, the new technology on offer, the hope with the music filtered in from abroad, filtered through Goa via the dargahs and temples, the riverbeds and the mountains, becoming Delhi's own. A small window of celebration and joy in the farmhouses and the disused spaces, before the police got wind of it and shut it down, before the moral panic set in. These parties broke the barriers and stormed the city for a while.

These were the places he went to in the night when I went home to Aunty and lay in bed wrapped up in our love. These are the places he went to dance, take acid, MDMA, where he thinks he is Shiva, Shiva in the flesh. Dancing this new reality, dancing the destruction and the chaos of the world. Everyone was delighted with him, he was well loved. He the one who never held back, who danced through the night like a shaman, a dervish, like a god. Who went on his hands and knees and howled, roared like a lion, tore off his clothes. He was famous for it.

I knew none of this. This part of his life he kept away from me, he didn't let me into this world, he wanted me all for himself. But for a time these people held the bloom of something new, something no one had seen here before. Like everyone who sees such things, they saw a new consciousness, the end of one world and the beginning of a more enlightened age.

*

He dresses her up in these clothes and it transforms him much more than her, he becomes hard, he's hard just watching her slip them on, a storm has risen in his eyes, the air has changed. It's not the girl that he desires, it's this possession of her, what he's made, the dressed-up thing. He puts her in front of the mirror, stands behind her, his hands around her waist, feeling across her, passing over every inch, rising to her ribs, beneath her breasts, under her arms, her shoulders, her neck, kisses her neck, slides his hands back down between her legs over the fabric. He watches her as he does this and she watches his hands. He says, Look at yourself. And she looks. Admire yourself, and she does.

Fall in love with yourself. This is you.

He talks about Shiva to me. He fully reveals this part of himself that had earlier only been hinted at, and which in its distant orbit had been charming, little more than an affectation. But Shiva, he says, is all. Shiva in his aspect as destroyer.

*

After I see his family I tell no one of his death. I give no sign. I carry on with my daily routine. My exam results arrive and despite everything they are good. In the absence of marriage offers it is agreed I should look for a job. On the surface it is as if nothing has happened. If I maintain this I will be a bright young girl.

But slowly things come back to me. They come in dreams at first, nightmares of him that are hard to place. I tell myself not to remember as I wake, but in the corner of my eye they remain.

*

He has something for her now: a few drops of acid left in a bottle in the fridge, a gift, wrapped in foil, kept in the dark, still potent, waiting for an occasion to be used.

. . .

He drops it on the back of my hand and I bring it to my mouth. He has another drop for himself. Now it's done there's no going back.

I've made my excuses with Aunty: I'm staying over at a friend's house. It's quiet in the colony. In the darkness outside good people have retreated to their beds, but we won't sleep. He says I'll see things tonight, the world will open up to me. I'll see it for the illusion it really is.

We leave the flat and go down to the car. He says we'll drive into the night out in the desert towards Jaipur.

Driving through the city, nothing happens for a long time. I say, Maybe it's not working, maybe we should take some more? And he laughs and says, Trust me, it's coming, you just have to wait.

. . .

It begins on the Gurgaon road. Yawning, each one suck-
ing in a lungful of air, but it's not tiredness, it's something else, as if bubbles are rising and the atoms of the
body are breaking loose. The buildings at the side tingle
and shudder. The tail-lights of cars leave tracers of red
in their wake. And in the belly, there's this feeling of but-
terflies, the compulsion to bring it all up, the impossibil-
ity of it, and the knowledge that if you could, it would
be nothing less than the universe, a projectile stream of
galaxies from the mouth.

But this is only a whisper, a small wave, it comes, it goes.
Relax, he says. Relax, and his voice comes to me from far
away. I close my eyes and focus on the dark throbbing
music he plays, the low hum of the engine. We're on the
highway in the desert.

I open my eyes to a carnivalesque world. Unhinged, the
trucks come roaring at us with their painted faces and
vicious mouths, the cheap flashing statues of neon gods
that adorn their dashboards leading the charge, dancing
into the void. Real objects slide on the surface of things.
Solid spaces bend. What I once knew to be true is only a

canvas to be painted on and torn apart. I turn to look at him and he's a black beast with a grinning maw. I can't help laughing out loud. I laugh at him for what seems like hours. There's a panic somewhere there.

On the stereo the sheer terror of Vivaldi.

Haunting corridors and cloisters, bales of straw across fields, sweat cooling on the skin.

She loses speech, hearing.

Her sense of self, always so certain, so fearful, begins to fall away. Her personality, so fixed and inevitable, reveals itself to be entirely open to change.

Here it peaks.

And then it breaks.

Like passing from a raging torrent into a vast and eerie lake.

He pulls the car over at a dhaba. The engine dies, the music stops. She can hear it ticking as it cools. The silence is unnerving. His face is watching hers; his eyes drift like coracles tied to the dock of his nose. He insists they go in.

She says she won't go in. He goes in. It's 3 a.m.

There's nothing left but the tremor of the tyres, the horns going off like ships leaving port, horns like the charges of matadors. In the trees the tube lights hang at odd angles, the broken limbs of angels. The insects of India swarm, drawn to the brightness that is a gas fogging the eyes.

He returns without a word and we are driving again. We might never have stopped. We drive for ever and turn around and drive back again.

We end in the birthing fields of Gurgaon, among those infinite constructions that have become ruined cities to me, the emptiness of history reflected in the stars above. I don't know how we got here, how much time has gone and what has been lost.

. . .

Ahead there is one building site framed by bamboo drenched in an artificial light with workers crawling across the concrete and steel.

They look like ants devouring an elephant's corpse. Only the corpse will devour the ants in the end, devour them and grow up tall.

We fall down before it, are silent in awe of it. He makes love to me on the desert floor. I see other faces in him; he changes before my eyes into an old man, a demon, a little boy. The birds circle around to pick at our bones.

Light falls from the sky, the stars fade, the horizon grows grey and real. The drug wears off, sadness leaves a mist. The men in the distance carry on their work, oblivious to any of this. We get in the car and drive back into Delhi without words. As the morning stirs I see men and women who have slept all night rise from their beds, enter the streets again, sweep the earth, go about their work. I thought I'd be free, released of my chains. Now I only see how it will end.

*

But oh! I'm meeting the NRI today. Oh sweetness and light and what joy! The day has finally arrived. He is here for me, my ticket to the Promised Land.

He's waiting in the coffee shop of the Taj Mansingh, he sees me and puts up his hand, recognizes me from the photo Aunty sent. He's buttoned up and bland, this American. Just like an American should be, in a lime-green polo shirt and chinos, side parting and perfect white teeth. A nice guy I'm sure, but at this point nice means nothing to me, I can barely tell if I'm awake or asleep, and I can only take so much of sweet.

Aunty laughs and trills like a bird of paradise when she's getting me ready to go. She's overseeing the game of dress-up we play. She's certain about this one now; she knows that he is the one for me.

. . .

He greets me like an old friend at the table. He clumsily tries to kiss me on the cheek. Tells me I'm much prettier in person than he imagined on the phone. We sit down and order nimbu-pani, but when it comes it's too sugary, so he sends it back and asks for a Diet Coke instead.

He complains about India awhile to me, about how slow and inefficient it is compared to the States, how customer service is zero here, how the taxi drivers don't know where to go. But he's almost signed the papers for a new apartment in Gurgaon. His parents are going to move there when they get old, back to the motherland, and there'll be a room for us there as well.

He places his palms on the table in an emphatic show. It's so good to finally meet you. He asks how college is going, and tells me he's been looking into courses around New York for me, advertising or marketing, a way to make use of my degree. He believes in a joint-income family after all.

. . .

I see his eyes on me, decent and dull, and I know what he wants from me, that he wants to turn me into a good girl. That he thinks he knows who I am.

I tell him I'd like to study film maybe.

And he says, Have you seen *American Beauty*? It's a masterpiece.

*

And even though he is dead I still call him on his phone. I sit in my room and I pick up my mobile to dial his number that I know by heart. Only his voicemail comes through, but his voice is beautiful on the line. He has a separate voice, one he puts on for this role. None of the madness is there. He's reasonable, perfectly calm.

The message isn't long. He says his name and the fact that he's not here right now, but he'll get back as soon as he can. In a deep and resonant voice. A voice full of easy confidence. A voice that doesn't match his animal face.

*

In August college restarted, my final year coming so abruptly upon us that the dream of the summer was at an end.

He said he'd do my work for me, write my essays, he'd do whatever, it was easy for him, he'd make sure I passed with the highest grades. I wouldn't have to do a thing.

In college, in the lectures, I look around at my classmates, at the girls who I've been out with before, whose fortunes had been read alongside mine, and I feel apart from them, superior, changed. I see the life they lead, the things they do, the direction they're heading in, and I want none of it. My old sadness is worn as a kind of arrogance now.

*

In bed, in the living room, driving in the car, it's much the same. He says, It's just you and me now, and I say, Yes, just you and me. No one else in the world. Fuck them, he says. Fuck everyone. We'll go crazy, we'll show them all. And I say, Yes, yes, we'll do it. Show them all.

He says it's time to leave that world behind, leave Aunty behind, leave marriage behind, leave society behind, and I say, Yes, yes. When he's inside me I say yes. He says, Move out of that house, move in here with me. And when he's inside me I say yes. I will. I'll go get my things, I'll tell her, I'll shock them all. He says, Do it, do it now, you don't need their hypocrite world any more, their safety, their ignorance, their preservation. You have me now. And I say, Yes.

It's a heady world of make-believe.

But I am a coward and I'll never leave.

*

A month passes from the day I hear of his death; I call his voicemail all the time. Ten, twenty times a day, I call him just to hear what he has to say, but it's always the same. Even as I'm going about my vacuumed life, I step aside and dial the number to hear the only part of him that remains.

· · ·

Out of hiding, almost imperceptibly, I begin to drive the city again. Routes are muscle memory and Delhi an extension of him. So I drive to the places we have been, grief-stricken but free. I drive the streets at night looking for him. I drive through Lutyens' Delhi. I go to the American Diner and drink a Bloody Mary alone.

*

We're sitting in the American Diner, me and him, drinking Bloody Marys, eating chili dogs. We've commandeered the Tabasco sauce. We sit on the stools at the bar, watch what's happening from here, keep an eye on the red-and-white Formica room, to the right of the cash register with the door behind. Good for conversation, good for getting little extras from the barman. Chili dogs, onion rings, Bloody Marys and later a glass of beer. Our glorious playground Delhi. He whispers in my ear.

A family comes in and sits at the far corner of the bar on the side that leads to the hotel exit. Father, mother, daughter. The girl is about fifteen. I see her right away and she sees me too. She's watching us, curious. I tell him this and he casts his eye over her. He leans into me and says, See, she's another you. The only difference is that she knows it already. It's true, you can see something in her, that curiosity, that restlessness, the disobedience. The arms so thin they might break, with that body and the long black hair, very straight, sitting erect and still as a coal in a fire. Her parents are nothing like her, their surfaces have dulled, and who's to say she won't dull too. But right now she's aflame. And we're staring at her.

We can't stare for ever. I tell him to watch me instead. He looks at me. But she knows she's been seen, that she's the object of our attentions, our curiosity. So there's the three of us now, watching, and no one else to know, and she's looking at me, asking telepathically, What are you doing with this monster by your side? And I'm saying to her, I don't know. But you should try it some time.

*

Delhi, yes.

Black bilgewater out of every orifice. Water flowing from the drainage channel. The cops have cordoned off the underpass from Lothian Road. Lothian Road to the

Red Fort, stray dogs are eating a corpse down there. They're using rocks to chase them away but the dogs don't scare, they keep coming back for more.

In September we take to walking after college, walking Old Delhi as the sun goes down. The monsoon has left its glory behind. This is the height of us. It will never be like this again.

We see another dead body here, before entering the old city at Mori Gate. He is leading me through the streets with him. I am letting myself be led. We're heading across from the slumber of Civil Lines where we've parked, heading from the red-brick charm of Court Road up to Mori Gate, past the police parade ground, up to the edge of the walled city. Each broken brick arch in the distance houses a person, a family, a way to stay alive, the alleyways beyond holding a million lives. People living here the way weeds live in ruins and make flowers. Millions of them, people in the mazes of alleys beyond, where the sun barely shines, through the gaps, with the temples and the minarets and churches, along paths that are labyrinthine. Inside the old city, there's the smell of engine oil, mechanics with their spare parts, with their shops for screws, brackets, car stereos, flashing lights. A wall of tyres stacked ten metres high, stinking of rubber, towards the Old Delhi station, obscuring the golden dome of St. James's Church. And kerosene, this is the smell of Delhi too. The gas burners for the bubbling oil, for the samosas and pakodas in their wide-bottomed pans. But in the crowds of open road before the old city this young man is dead. Dead, face up on the pavement, whose cobbles have shaken loose as if they've been through an earthquake.

You can see it from far off. There's something unmistakable, entirely separate from sleep. From drunkenness or unconsciousness. This young man, this Raju, bus passenger, cheap groper, son to a mother, friend, thief, piece of meat. In his early twenties maybe, he's clean-shaven and not long dead, wearing a black plastic jacket. Cheap and dead with no tale to tell. The mouth, as you get closer, it's been ripped open on the left side, torn as if caught on a fishing line so it gives an awful grin of skeletal teeth behind the veil of cheek. And the eyes are wide open, staring up in disbelief. Soon the crows will have them, they'll pluck them out. There are only socks on his feet.

His shoes are gone. Someone must have already stolen them.

Everyone is walking around him, acting as if he isn't there. Thousands of feet, no one seems to notice. We keep walking too. He says, Look, don't stop, there's nothing else to do. A cop is directing traffic down on the Tis Hazari road. We all know not to approach him, he'll happily take us in, question us, come up with an absurd theory, some trumped-up charge. Why are you so interested in a dead man? What does it have to do with you?

My memory always enters Old Delhi at Mori Gate. No matter where I am, it enters into this maze from here, which I have learned through him by heart. Into the medieval stone and commerce, and the din of daily voices in their treble shriek, words swamped by film songs on old radios, battered TV sets and the urgency of porters with heavy loads yelling for people to get out of their way.

. . .

Through this maze and out into descending night to the scene of Hamilton Road, past the queues of cycle rickshaws and the toilet blocks, and families with young girls in make-up and cheap clothes, over the railway bridge, just like a fairground, the colour and bustle, the ephemeral joy of the lit-up. A dentist is sitting cross-legged waiting for customers, kept company by pliers and a pile of orphaned teeth on the side of the road.

Into the bazaar north of Chandni Chowk we plunge, to the market inhabiting the centuries-old stone, plastic toys, calculators, computers and games, stationery, manuals. Everything you could hope to find has its place here, junk piled up high into rooms which tiptoe into blackness, passageways that fork and vanish into crypts, double back on themselves. Above ground or underground, inside or out, it's unclear.

We emerge without warning into the pavement of Chandni Chowk. He pulls me across a gap in the road, past the cycle rickshaws. The Red Fort is glowering at one end. The sound of so many bodies swallowing us. And the fort is gone.

. . .

Then a measure of peace, a side alley where nothing stirs. Turning back you can see people marching past the crack of it. It happens like this sometimes, some lanes remain forever hidden away.

He walks me deeper into the walled city, twisting down narrow passageways and alleyways, knowing the way by heart. Suddenly we're in the place where lives are spent behind walls, in courtyards where the walls are front doors. It's where the Muslim girls roam, in twos and threes, heavenly girls of milk-white whose skin the sun does not see—they glide past us in silence with their painted cat eyes framed in black.

Turning into another alleyway, he slows our pace to follow a pair moving arm in arm ahead. Suddenly I see them with his eyes, feel his obscene desire, the sport he makes of them. My sisters and me. Because I love him we follow them like this, see their sashaying walk, seek the plaited hair peeking below the waist. Beneath the blackness of their outer world there are gaudy colours, there are sequined and embroidered clothes of pink and blue, pierced ears and noses, rings and studs, necks clamped in jewels, arms in bangles, legs in anklets, feet in heels. I taste the hunger he has for them, for their enormous kohl eyes etched in black, for their lips made up with ruby-red and lashes rising to the moon.

Somewhere, behind closed doors, in cramped and barren rooms, in happy rooms of austere stone, they'll lie down in their splendour and a man will make love to them, beat them for a look or a word, for no reason at all, will despise them, ignore them, be blind to them, somewhere someone will caress them, whisper secrets in their ears, buy gifts to appease them, make them smile, coax a laugh from their lips from which love trickles like a brook. Her eyelids open and close in the heat of the night, overlooking the masjid.

In his room we hold Old Delhi inside us, the things we've seen: the torn cheek, the teeth, the clicking heel on stone, the fleeting eye, the hair beneath the veil. He talks it to me, he fucks me slowly with his words, takes his pain out on me from the city he's consumed, merging limbs and lips, doing it to me again and again. I beg him. He wraps his hands around my throat and sinks inside. He wants to be with me everywhere, wants to follow me through the streets. I'd walk for him and he'd obliterate me, take everything but my eyes. I'd cover myself, in devotion, and know that I was owned.

*

But it's the same old problem, the one we come back to every time. He says, Leave, move in with me, and I say I will . . . but I can't. I ask him to wait awhile and he says, What for? He gets angry and stalks the apartment, calls me a liar, a coward, drinks some more, says I'm boring, just like everyone else. He wonders why he's wasting his time. I'm a tease and a tourist. He becomes angry because I leave, because of the way I guard myself, the way I never let go, as if I've learned nothing from him. But it's OK. He'll show me if it kills him, he'll carry me kicking and screaming through his world.

Driving home I feel everything that's been lost, I feel the sudden fear of a life out of control, knowing it's too late to go back and that I've already gone too far. Going home I think how I can escape, how I can get away from what we've done. And then I get inside Aunty's static world and I can't wait to run back to him.

*

Under the pretext of looking for jobs I drive around the city all the time, spend hours driving around in my car alone. Then go to his apartment and sit outside and look, waiting for something to happen.

Finally something does happen: a family appears, a smart-looking corporate type with his wife and small child. I watch them on the balcony and through the living room window from the dark of my car. I keep coming back for more. I watch the husband leave for work in the morning. I watch the wife standing on the balcony as he goes.

A few days later his voicemail dies.

*

In Nizamuddin I ring the bell of the apartment door. The maid answers and I ask to speak to sir or madam, knowing that sir has already left for work.

. . .

Madam comes to the door holding her young child, a curious look on her face. I act surprised to see her, as if expecting someone else. I ask her right away where they are, if the family is in or away. She tells me they don't live here any more, they sold the apartment, it only happened two weeks ago, it was a very quick sale. Oh, I say, but I've come all the way from Chandigarh. I'd lost their number but I knew the house, I used to live just round the corner and now . . . Do you have a number for them? Do you know where they've gone?

She says she'll get it for me, would I like to come in?

The woman offers me a seat in the living room while she goes to leave her child with the maid. The Japanese screen doors have been removed—now family photos cover the walls. It's hard to believe it's the same home.

She comes back and sits down opposite and asks me what I'm doing here in Delhi, besides coming to find old friends. I tell her I'm applying for my visa to the States, and also meeting a boy who I might be marrying, who's from the U.S. himself. He's only here for a few days, but we've met six times before and I think he might be the one. The lies fall out my mouth very easily. But it's hard being here. Beneath the layers of new furniture and everyday life I can see where I've been ripped apart.

She sees my wandering eye and asks, It must look different to you. I heard their son did a lot of work on it in the last few years. Did you know him very well?

I say I knew him a long time ago when we were small, he was older than me, he used to tease me a lot, but when we moved to Chandigarh we lost touch.

She nods and says, So you really haven't heard? Well, I hate to be giving such bad news, but he died, not so long ago at all. He fell in front of a truck on the highway. He was drunk. It was in the papers, they said it was suicide and a girl was involved, but then there usually is in these cases, no? She drove him to it, that's what they say. It almost stopped us buying the place, but since he didn't actually die here we thought that there's really no bad luck involved.

·   ·   ·

The pain is suddenly very sharp, like a clockwork razor turning in my chest; I feel it tightening and cutting me to shreds. I want to run away from here as fast as I can. I ask if I may use the bathroom instead.

As soon as I shut the door my strength begins to fail. I have to cover my mouth with my hands to stop myself from crying out. When I look around me, I see that nothing in this room has changed. There's the same chipped tiles, the cracking paint on the pipes, the plaster falling from the walls, the same shower, the frosted glass with the sunlight seeping in. I see my face in the mirror and I know that one day I will die. Slowly, with great effort, I pull my breathing back, take deep inhalations and in the warmth and the whiteness I close my eyes. I am alive.

*

He says, Open your eyes. Open your fucking eyes. Don't be blind your whole life. Don't be blind to it. Open them up. I open them and he's looking down at me, flaring in the sun.

*

In October it finally began to come apart. The Israelis moved down to Delhi from the mountains, on their way back to Sinai, to Tel Aviv, on their way to the new season in Goa. This great pack of Israelis coming into Paharganj. They called him up from there. They needed him to fix some things.

I didn't know it then but he was going out most nights. Going out to smoke, drink, shoot up. In rooms with strangers and friends. Waiting for me to come back to him in the day. But getting bored of me. In rooms with men just like Franklin John.

*

I learned all this from K.

K the fat Buddha man, one of the greatest dealers Delhi's ever known. Dark like my love, but unlike him possessed of a beatific face, a face that catches the light, without malice, a face to put your faith into. Self-taught, home-grown, raised right out of the dirt of Orissa, unable to read or write, but he could speak seven languages, he learned Hebrew in three months. He knew everyone.

. . .

K sat in all of his hotel rooms and the models came, the designers came, the actors and actresses came, the sons of politicians came. They all shook his hand, venerated him. They came to talk, hang out, pick up what they needed, and he sat there like a maharaja with his cigar, the centre of the world. When his customers arrived he'd have a long chat, he'd reach into the bag by his side, take out the drug, give a little more from his own supply, give it on credit if required, always with a good word and a smile.

K was an acquaintance of his, not quite a friend, both part of the scene. We were introduced in a five-star hotel suite at the very start of things, in those glorious first three weeks. We'd gone to pick up some money he was owed. Downstairs in the hotel a fashion show was going on. K was keeping everyone high above.

When we went into the hotel suite that day K looked him up and down, gave a wry smile and shook his hand. He said he hadn't seen him in a long time, but that he was looking well.

. . .

I was introduced but we didn't stay long. We picked up the money and left. But K shook my hand then and quietly handed me his card as I walked out the door.

*

Outside the flat in Nizamuddin, with the woman watching me from the balcony above, I searched the glove box for K's card. It was there, buried under papers, off-white and expensively made. I had no one else to talk to then, nowhere else to go any more. No voice to hear on the phone. I drove awhile until I was away from there, parked in a small street in Lodhi Colony and then called.

K answered the phone almost right away. He said, Hello and nothing more. In the silence that followed I told him who I was and where we'd met before. He said he remembered me and he was sorry because he'd heard the news. Would I like to come over to see him some time? He said he was in the Meridien, he gave me the number of the suite, said he'd be around for a while.

. . .

I sat with him for a few hours that same day, nestled in a couch at the side of the room, listening to him talk. He said how much I'd changed. He remembered a fresh and nervous college girl.

Between customers, between answering the phone, he talked to me, talked about things absent-mindedly, talked about his business, kept me occupied. When the customers came I sat alone at the side and watched until they were gone. Finally he came round to the only thing I wanted to know. He said he was not at all surprised by what happened, that he always thought it would end this way, that he was a wild one, that no one could live like he did for so long and not come crashing down to the ground. He told me all about the parties, about the raves.

*

For a week or so I go back to K, day after day, and he tells me the things he knows. I listen to it all. I keep coming back. He doesn't mind, he says I'm good luck for him. I sit in the room while he conducts his business. I provoke curiosity in his customers. I sit there every day, numbed somehow and lost in thought. He asks me what I'm going to do with myself now. I say I don't know. I've finished college, I was thinking of getting a job. Where I live, they're getting impatient, but they've given up trying to marry me off.

At some point he looks over at me as if I've been noticed for the first time. He cuts a couple of lines of coke, holds out a rolled-up banknote and says I should help myself. He says it'll make me feel better.

There's nothing in the world like the first line of cocaine. The way it hits the brain, sharpens the lights of the room, removes all doubt, removes the pain. Removes guilt too.

I take two grams with me. He says there's no rush to pay, just go, forget about him, enjoy yourself. That's what he would have done. There's a whole city out there waiting for you.

I do another line in the room and then I drive back home.

*

Throughout our love, until it was much too late, there was always the hope that he would change. That he would become rich, successful, respectable. Respectable above all else, because of his ideas and the wealth they would bring. That one day he would become rich on his own, not through inheritance but through talent, skill, that he would make money, make business, do something. That this would be enough for me to present him to my family and say, Look, I found someone. And if he were rich, if he were famous, if he were a recognized success, if they knew him from the papers, if he had been confirmed in some public way, then they would embrace him. They would overlook his flaws, his ugliness, his black skin, his well of madness. They would be happy to let me go to him. All the way through I held on to a hope like this, like the coward that I was. I could never quite let that go.

*

I went to the qawwalis one more time. I got out of the car and walked down the path to the same alleyway past the mosque, shining bright with all those godly lights.

But it was cramped and noisy and I was painfully alone and it stank of men and their meat and their eyes.

Still inside the dargah, by the shrine, I hoped for some of the old magic to appear, for the music to lift me, for the saint to return the love I once gave. But the saint kept his distance and the music left me cold. It was tone-less, an empty edifice behind a veil in a world built by fools.

I stood as I used to stand, not knowing what to do with myself. The way the devotees behaved, it seemed more like a train station than a holy place. Men went into the shrine like a ticket office as the women and children huddled together outside. They stared morosely, nudg-ing, gossiping, scowling. I looked around the empty space trying to hold on to something, but it wasn't the same. I saw things I hadn't noticed, the dirty stains on the marble, the ugly white lights and the shops on the edges selling bright, tawdry clothes. I smelled the ripe-ness of armpits and unwashed feet and became full of hate. I despised it all.

. . .

All eyes seemed to fall on me, the women's more than ever. They were watching, sniggering, twisting their lips. Making me feel foolish and ashamed. Because I was alone, because of the way I was dressed. I couldn't take being watched like this so I went to the edge of the courtyard away from the music and stood at the wall in the shadows thinking I would be all right there. But there other pious women began to notice, to hiss at me, curse me for leaning against the wall, for doing things I didn't even know were wrong. And when I stepped forward and squatted down to try to hide they hissed at me some more.

I retreated from the dargah back to my car. I cursed them all the way. I drove a short distance until I reached Jor Bagh, parked and cut myself a line, then drove through the city at speed.

*

Him and me, we are driving up to Majnu ka Tila in October. The prayer flags are fluttering over the stagnant Yamuna breeze. He's picked me up from college to drag me here, called me out of the blue.

Rain came down for a day yesterday, out of season, surprising us all, bringing up the sewage and leaving the heat behind, and the flies and mosquitoes and the traffic fumes. Here by the refugee colony, old metal coaches are parked full of Tibetans, young men, young women, old men and women, all weighed down with boxes of supplies and possessions, waiting to head back up to the mountains. Foreigners too, sitting exhausted with their backpacks and matted hair by the side of the road, and the tangle of prayer flags over everything.

Inside the colony we walk through the alleys, past Internet cafés and travel agents. In a guest house there's a long-haired Tibetan from Amdo called Losel, who dresses like a basketball player, speaks American English and has fifty tolas of charas he's looking to get rid of.

He grins at us in the murky restaurant with four cheap marble tables. There's the smell of fried food and incense. Next to him a stocky monk is slurping noodle soup, dripping sweat from the end of his nose. His arms are tree trunks, and although the rest of his body is hidden within the crimson robes, you can feel the strength of it, the kind of strength that pulls trucks in its wake and lifts rubble. He has a wiry moustache and goatee and a hairline low on his head.

Losel puts an arm around the monk's shoulders, saying, This is my brother. The monk stops eating, turns his head towards Losel and curls his lip, the kind of sneer that's reserved for a cockroach. Then Losel says something in Tibetan and the monk produces a great grin that transforms his face and continues eating.

He hates it here, Losel says, addressing me, gripping the monk's shoulder even tighter. He thinks Delhi is a hell and I've become one of its demons. He's only here for a night to pick up supplies, but even this is too much. He thinks the city is evil, it gives him a headache, dealing with the dishonest people, the liars and the thieves. He's from Amdo, just like me. We came together over the mountains, eight of us through the snow walking single file at night from Amdo through Tibet to Nepal and then here. It took eight weeks—hiding in the day, walking at night. They have the snipers up there. It was OK though, no problem, no one died that time. One of us died later but he had TB. Two more are in prison now.

Losel was seventeen when he left home. His mother was worried he'd end up dead, or worse, Chinese. He didn't want to leave at first, he liked it up there. But he got into too much trouble. Squabbling over an unpaid debt he blew up a Muslim bookie's car. He made a petrol bomb of the gas tank and blew that old BMW into the sky. His mother sent him away the next day.

The monk interrupts him, begins talking, talks fast and stern, as if he's lecturing. He goes on like this for a while and Losel gives him short replies, starts to laugh, until the monk bangs his fist on the table, gets up and walks away. Losel watches him go. He says, He worries about my soul. He's going upstairs to watch people killing each other on STAR Movies. He likes the action films best of all.

*

We drive down from Majnu ka Tila to the Tibetan Monastery Market. Through the flyover arch we walk to the stalls of clothes surrounded by college students. Left before the main market, past the bell of the monastery—there's a small alleyway, nothing more than a gutter between two buildings, on either side of which there are more shops selling bags and shoes and all manner of counterfeit clothes. At the end of that alley, dodging the sewage running through the middle, we come to a door with panels painted black so you can't see inside. Into that drab building, through another door on the right, and you're in Tibet.

The room is a great dark canteen full of noise and incense, twelve tables of monks and laymen all together, photos of the Dalai Lama on the walls alongside a giant photograph of Lhasa from the air. High in one corner, a TV is screeching, half the room absorbed in its boom bang, the other half in conversation—loud, intense, spirited—or eating. Monks gobble noodles. We sit at the only empty table and Losel orders Coca-Cola, thentuk, phing sha, fried beef momos.

.   .   .

They begin to talk about the charas, how good it is, where he got it from, what the price should be. He says he'll sell for three hundred, you can sell it on for six. Who's buying?

There are some Israelis in Paharganj, they're waiting for it right now, they called last night.

Coming from?

Old Manali—some are heading to Goa, some of them are going home. They want to take it back with them too.

At the end of the meal we leave the monks and the smoke and go back down the alleyway, back into the market, inside one of the countless shops, up some step-ladders in the back to a storeroom above the ceiling, full of shoeboxes. A pretty young Tibetan girl is sleep-ing, Losel shakes her awake. My wife, he says. She stretches and yawns. Without a word she pulls out one of the shoeboxes, pushes it towards us and goes back to sleep. Fifty tolas inside, creamy little pellets wrapped in cling film.

Losel passes him one, he peels the film off, scratches it with his nail, sniffs, nods, throws it back again. He takes the envelope from his pocket, counts out fifteen thou-sand and hands it over.

*

The Israelis are waiting for us on the roof terrace of Anoop Hotel. They don't stay here, it's just the meet-ing place. The Israelis. Most of them are just out of the army, muscled, tattooed, letting their hair grow long—the women as tough and free as the men.

Others are scared of them, and they keep to themselves, they don't mix well, they move in packs, don't suffer fools. But they love him. They think he's a crazy one, this crazy Indian coming into their world, talking with them as one of their own, talking with a brain, charm-ing them. Not like the others, not trying to suck up and serve. He wears a Star of David when he meets them. They love him for this too. They laugh. They say maybe he's one of them, he could be one of the lost tribe.

And they hate Delhi. Another reason to love him. He makes the city bearable for them. They call him up on the phone and he makes it better, he knows where to get hold of the best charas, the best dope, the Valium and ketamine from the corrupt pharmacies.

The room we go to is like Franklin's. Mosquito blood-stains on the walls, sewer stench lingering, incense burn-ing. In the process of packing, unpacking or repacking, someone's belongings got scattered about the place. There are drums and chillums and dirty clothes, and a machete on the bed.

Ten of them are standing there. The bed is cleared, fifty tolas are spread out on the mattress. One is opened up, passed around, inspected by everyone. Guarded smiles and shrugs and nods, a ripple of cautious approval, and someone begins to crumble charas into a mixing bowl.

The negotiations begin. He starts at eight hundred per tola and they baulk at this, laugh at him. They say, Come on, man, be real. He laughs back, gives nothing away, declares the provenance, says it's from Malana itself, reminds them that he's the trustworthy one and they came to him, he's not a dirty Kashmiri, he's not like the others on the street. He says they won't find anything this good on their own, not here, not for this much, not now. Go out in the street and ask for it, see what they give you. So they offer five. He looks offended, goes to collect the charas in the shoebox like a kid gathering his toys. They laugh at him and push him away and say, OK, OK. Make it six, and he looks at them with raised eyebrows and shakes his head and says, Seven five. Six, they repeat. He makes as if to spit on the floor, pauses, grins, says, OK, six five.

Six five. There's a discussion about it. Good enough.

Thirty-two thousand, rounded down.

*

Smoke in the room now, everyone getting blasted, chillums being smoked empty, cleaned with cloth that's torn into strips, repacked, bom Shiva, lit. One of the men picks up the machete from the bed. He says it belonged to another guy, another Israeli, not in their group though, a guy who smoked too much, didn't have the right head, had a bad temper, cracked. They were at the beach one morning after a party, it was in Goa at the start of April, the season was ending, the music was still playing in the jungle not far away, and this guy, he was sitting at the edge of this group in the sand, spaced out, coming down. And then this cow . . . This cow is behind him, coming towards him, trying to get into his bag, you know, poking its head around, flicking out its tongue, the flies are around it. He has some food in his bag. The cow wants the food. This guy is pushing it away, cursing it, pushing it with his hands, but every time he pushes it, it just keeps coming back again. And this guy is getting angrier and angrier. His, how do you say? His patience, you know, it's not so good.

People in the room start to laugh.

So what does he do? His temper goes, OK. He gets up, he's had enough, he empties his bag on to the sand, dumps everything out, everything in his bag, and looks at the cow and he shouts at it, in Hebrew, he's saying, Go on then, fucker, eat it. Eat everything. And the cow, it just keeps going on, doesn't know what he's saying, it keeps coming forward and starts eating. There is some banana, a piece of bread. And everyone around is laughing. Everyone thinks it's fucking funny, you know. But what else is in the bag? This fucking machete. So what does he do? He picks up the machete. It's also on the ground. Boom. He puts it into the fucking cow's neck. Right into its fucking neck. This guy's crazy, you know. He puts the machete right into the neck. Crack. You see the bone and the meat and the blood. Blood everywhere. Everyone who was laughing, now they're jumping up from the sand. What the fuck? Are you crazy, man? But he keeps going. He's taking the head off, there's blood everywhere. There are locals on the beach, fishermen, chai sellers. They're all watching this. They're not happy. Oh no. And before you know what's happening, a crowd is forming, they're watching this like they don't believe their fucking eyes. This cow is fucking dead and everyone else is backing away from him and he's there with the cow. Then he kind of, you know, wakes up, he looks around. There's this dead cow on the ground and he's standing there and these locals are all staring at him. This guy is thinking, Fuck.

People start laughing in the room.

And he's running. Running for his life. There's all these locals after him, and they've got knives and machetes and sticks and he's running away from the beach, towards the trees, he's gone over the bushes, into the trees, and the locals are charging after him. He vanished. Never seen anyone run so fast, not even in the middle of a war. We never saw him again.

. . .

Now he holds the machete in the air, touches the chillum to his forehead. Says, Cow-killing machete motherfucker.

*

With coke in my blood and my brain I take to driving fast into the night. I drive through Lutyens' Delhi. The thrill of a straight road, of regular street-lights ticking like a metronome, the steady purr of the engine, changing down gears, suddenly coming to a stop at the red light. Two men pull up alongside me on a bike.

They look inside the car. I know the wild excitement they must feel when they see me alone in here. The bike's engine revs. And the light is still red. So do I drive? Do I look at them? The last thing I should do is look at them. I turn my head and I look at them. As soon as I do their eyes widen in pleasure and the passenger grips the rider's waist, holds him and says something into his ear. The bike veers away in a loop. It loops to the left, off behind me, and it pulls back louder and faster a moment later alongside my driver's window.

Like a kennel of dogs they howl and bang on the glass with the palms of their hands. Then the pillion rider tries to open the door.

Although the light is still red, I put my foot down on the gas. I'm screeching off, along Akbar Road towards India Gate. The motorbike does the same, following me at speed, racing with me, pulling up alongside my window, dipping behind, flashing its lights and beeping the horn, and I can hear the men wailing on top of it. The road ahead is empty, the wide road deserted, shrouded by the overhanging trees—I accelerate into it.

Around India Gate they're still on me. I twist round Tilak Marg and accelerate hard out of the bend. A few cars pass on the other side. Ahead at the crossroads by the Supreme Court the light is red. I see the bike coming to my side and jerk towards it, forcing it to brake. Then

I take my chance and floor it, drive straight through the light and the traffic.

Behind, in the mirror, I watch the bike being hit by a car side-on at speed, a police van far behind with flashing lights, and the bike and the men spilling out on the road.

*

I dreamed of him last night, and in the dream he came back to life. He didn't even know that he'd been dead. It's the guilt that's doing this to me I suppose, the guilt of resurrecting him. Of making him over, using his likeness and sculpting him like a piece of clay.

In the dream he's following me around, all over Delhi, begging me to take him back, like a fool, to let him be with me. He looks exactly as he did, the same clothes and hair, the same age. But he is calmer. Infinitely sadder because of this.

.   .   .

He doesn't remember the things he's done so he can't understand why I won't have him. He begs me, he's close to tears. I feel pity for him. I try to let him down gently, tell him it's impossible. I don't have the heart to tell him he's been dead, that more than ten years have passed. He doesn't seem to notice that I'm older than him now. He seems so ordinary, without power. And he continues to beg all the while, hands wrung. He says, I won't make a sound, I'll be by your side, I'll follow you everywhere, make you happy, do anything you say.

*

We leave the Israelis at midnight. He has a weight behind his reddened eyes. He drives around in silence, we drive through the night and he drinks and he smokes and he drives, but he doesn't talk to me and he won't let me go home. I fall asleep in the car. I don't know what I've done wrong.

Then it's light outside, men are clearing their throats, retired colonels are taking their morning walks. I'm sure they can see me, that they all know. We drive and we park and we climb upstairs to go home.

. . .

Once inside he goes straight to the computer, sits there in silence typing away, talking in a chat room, looking at porn, drinking the whole time, smoking joint after joint. He doesn't look at me, still doesn't talk. I stand in the middle of the living room waiting for him to speak, but he doesn't speak. I go to bed and hug the pillow and try to sleep.

When I wake he's sitting at my side with a bottle of whisky in his hand.

He looks at me tenderly and strokes my face. He says, You're just like a stupid fucking college girl.

I pull the sheets around me and turn away. I tell him to leave me alone, ask him why he has to drink all the time. He only gets up and walks back outside.

I go out and he's on his computer again.

What are you doing?

He doesn't reply.

I go towards him and he puts his hand on the monitor switch. When I get close enough he switches it off so I can't see what he's been looking at.

He turns to face me and smiles.

I slap his face. I slap it again, I punch his arms and chest and pull at his hair. He watches me and just smirks. I tire, I'm suddenly exhausted, so I sit down on the sofa, and when I do he switches the monitor on again.

Enraged by this I storm over to him. I lift the monitor in my arms and threaten to throw it to the floor, the whole thing. I'll do it, I say. Don't try to stop me.

He looks at me and says that he won't. So go ahead. Do it. Go on.

I say I will. I'll do it right now.

Do it then. Go on.

I make a motion to throw it down but he doesn't react.

There are tears in my eyes.

He says, I'm waiting. Do it.

I don't do it. I can't. Instead I put it down and get my bag and head to the door. When I'm out and halfway down the marble stairs he calls out to me from above. I look back up to see him standing at the apartment door, smiling at me strangely, wires trailing behind him, the monitor in his arms.

His smile wilts as he lifts and then hurls the monitor through the air. It smashes by my feet on the ground.

*

The NRI rejected me too, after all was said and done. No reason was given, his family only made their polite excuses to Aunty on the phone. She was troubled, defeated. She said then that it was over, she had tried her best, she had always done what was right, but enough was enough. Now it would be better if I graduated and found a job, and maybe with a job I could look for another place to live.

*

The first man I pick up is in the coffee shop of the Claridges hotel. I've given up our old places. Given up the apartment with those people inside. There's nothing left of him but me. I want to go where we have no memory.

. . .

He's German, sandy blond and blue-eyed, almost a stereotype, with a face that's unmemorable and is saved only by his clothes, which give him a pardonable air of wealth. He must be in his late thirties—a powder-blue shirt and cream linen suit. He walks in and he's waiting to collect a cake for someone's birthday party, a niece maybe, or the daughter of a friend. Or maybe his own child. The cake is pink. While he's waiting for it to be packed he's starting to look around the room. I've been watching him from my table since he walked in, looking to be looked at. He sees me, makes eye contact for a moment, turns away. It's not five seconds before he comes back again.

Because I've continued to look, he decides to come over to the table. He approaches casually, asks if he can sit down while he waits. He's very polite. I tell him he can do as he likes. Now I see the tan line of his absent wedding ring.

Adjusting himself in his seat, he asks me where I'm from, and when I say I'm from Delhi he acts surprised.

He says he's never met a girl from Delhi like me, he thought I was a tourist. It's hard to speak to girls here, he says. His cake is brought to the table but he makes no effort to leave. I sit and let him talk. He tells me he's on a business trip, that he works as an analyst in corporate finance and he's often in Delhi and Bombay, sometimes in Bangalore.

He spends an unnecessary half hour talking me into bed with him, trying to impress me with self-deprecating humour, with innocuous joking barbs followed by earnest praise. Are you here alone? Did you drive here today? I bet you're a terrible driver, aren't you? I bet you crash all the time. No, really, I'm sure you're far better than me on these roads.

This kind of thing.

Delivered in a German monotone.

It's all very dull, very by the book. He tells me I have beautiful eyes. Finally he asks if I'm a guest here. No, I reply, I was just sitting, having a coffee on my way to see a friend.

· · ·

It excites him that I'm from the city. He thinks he has to make a special effort with me, he thinks he has to tread carefully, he has a rare chance, and a thing for brown skin. He tells me he has a room here in the hotel and he has to go out later for this function, but he's enjoyed talking to me, maybe I'd like to have a drink with him beforehand? I keep him waiting a moment, then smile and say, Why not? Encouraged, but not without trepidation, he asks if I'd also maybe like to come to his room.

We walk through the lobby and along the corridor side by side in a guillotine silence. As soon as we're inside he's fumbling at me, holding his hands to my waist, pressing his thin lips into mine, pushing me against the door, moving me towards the bed. Detached, out of my body, I let him do all this without a word. I begin to remove my clothes, and lie down on the bed. I let him do it to me and his breath is vile. When he's finished he climbs off without a word, goes into the bathroom. He's still there when I put on my clothes and walk out the door.

*

The next day he disappeared. I turned up at his apartment to find the door locked and the locks changed and his phone switched off. There was an air of finality about it.

Still I banged on the door and rang the bell, waited for an hour, calling his number over and over. I sat outside in my car another two hours before giving up and driving home.

Every day that he's gone I turn up at his apartment, for ten days I call his phone and it's the same, the apartment is locked, the phone dead. There's no one to speak to, nowhere to go. I feel completely alone. I drive past his place every morning before I go to college, in limbo, undone.

On the tenth day he calls me, casual as anything, saying he's home, asking to know where I am, why aren't I coming over? No explanation, nothing. No acknowledgement he's been away, been unreachable. Come over, he says. I tell him I can't, it's too late. I ask where he's been and he just murmurs. His voice has a strange, hollow edge.

When I turn up at his flat the next day there's a Star of David hanging above the outer door, and inside a giant UV painting of Shiva on the wall. He has Ali with him now. Ali is the one who answers the door. Just like that. He appears, his new companion. Ali lets me in. He seems to know who I am.

Ali is a good man, he's loyal to a fault, but he likes his drink as much as anyone else. He leads me into the living room, to where his master is. I point at Ali and say, Who's this? And as if it's the most obvious thing in the world he says, It's Ali. No clarification, no smile.

We sit in silence for half an hour, the three of us, Ali embarrassed and ashamed in front of me. He pours himself drink after drink. I see him suddenly. I see that his face is bloated, unrecognizable to me. I get up to leave and he grabs my arm. I pull myself away.

*

I meet the Businessman in September in the bar of the Taj Mansingh. It seems I am drawn to this place. Half an hour later I'm in a suite taking off my clothes.

Seated at the bar, I know I'm being watched. I've taken to sitting in these hotel bars in the afternoons with a drink in my hand, perched on the bar stool, my face perfectly calm. It's always peaceful at this hour, but then the men come over to me soon enough. Vulgar men, fat and rich men, drunk men, the sons of men. Delhi is rotten with the sons of men. I rarely even look at them. Sometimes they become angry and insult me.

But the Businessman is different. He's watching with distance, trying to place me, to work out what I'm doing here. I watch his reflection in the mirror behind the bar, see myself there too. He's in his late thirties. Handsome, well dressed, some grey forming on his temples, lines appearing on his once-smooth forehead. Wide eyes slightly downturned on a beautiful face, giving a melancholy look. A narrow nose, a pretty mouth, already some stubble after shaving. A youth misspent, callow and privileged, but not without its own pain.

He's been groomed for a life of power. But he has another power that is not the same as wealth and privilege, something inscrutable, a trick of genes or God, a power that exists parallel to the one that all these men have. He doesn't rush it. There's no threat anywhere. I see this in the way the barman brings him his drink with cautious respect, and the way he accepts it as if this is the most natural thing, without thanks or apology. He looks at me in the mirror.

I light a cigarette. The barman brings an ashtray for me. The Businessman lights one himself. I already know what will happen next. It's something we can feel easy about. So I smile in the mirror. The room is dim and quite empty in the afternoon.

He walks over, asks very properly if I'm waiting for someone. No, I reply. No one.

In that case would I mind if he sits?

I say I don't mind.

He raises his hand for the barman to bring him another drink.

But you're not a guest. He says it as a statement instead of a question, as a fortune-teller might.

No.

He waits for me to go further and when I don't he smiles and smells the whisky he's been served, brings it to his lips. We look at one another in the mirror.

He's a Delhi man, that's for sure, though not the kind Aunty dreamed of. He sips his drink and looks at me. He says, What are you doing here?

Nothing, just sitting, killing time. There aren't many places to sit in the city.

He asks where I'm from.

I say I'm from here.

Am I in college?

I've just finished. Now I'm looking for work.

In the suite we stand and look at one another for a long time. I go into the bathroom for a line. It's nothing like love or desire. Just the urge to destroy.

. . .

I make sure he knows nothing of my life. I remain a mask to him, superior. He says he can't understand where I've come from, that I'm a dream turned into flesh.

*

September 11. Everyone remembers what they were doing this day. I was with the Businessman in a hotel room, fucking, doing coke. He takes his shoes off and places them neatly at the side near the minibar. The lights are low, the plate-glass window shrouded with a curtain like the kind covering a stage. Lutyens' Delhi is outside, cars forever going round the traffic circles. The TV is on, the sound turned down, and night is coming upon us. We come to this room and fuck for hours. We are doing this, he is trying to possess me, climb into me, open me up, but he can't, however hard he tries. And then the towers are on TV, collapsing, and everything stops.

*

I meet him two or three times a week. In hushed hotels in the daylight I become his girl. He calls me to the room, leaves it for me when we are done. Nothing attached to it, no demands, though he likes to bring me expensive clothes, diamond earrings, more cocaine. Cocaine that strips the world away. Pares it to a point, trims off all fat, increases pleasure, numbs my pain. No past, no future. All inwardness gone. And a thirst like no other to consume.

*

One night he takes me out to Gurgaon and shows me what he is building there. He says it is the future and he owns it all.

*

His wealth is immense. It weighs on him sometimes. He tells me things about the land he's acquired, the real estate that he holds, the luxury apartment complexes, the miles and miles that are being built. His father is a failed man, a gambler, hot-headed and paranoid, he made rash deals in the past, almost lost everything the family owned. But he sent his son to study in Europe, and when his son returned he went to work building the business again, ruthlessly, brick by brick. Luck had played a part, the right place at the right time, but after that it was skill, talent, willpower, hard work. A certain lack of morals. He talks about the things that have to be managed, police and politicians, how every party must be appeased, groomed, positioned on the board, how bribes must be paid, how rivals have to be disappeared or destroyed, how every day is harder than the last, how there's never any peace, how life is war. I say nothing, I make no judgement at all.

The hotel room is hushed and sealed. The AC is on. It's 4 p.m. I undress. Stand naked above him.

Now the sun has risen outside and all the coke is gone, her mind is clogged, has reached the point of saturation, can go no higher. But she still tries, searches for every packet, looking for one that might have been missed, fingering the insides of the empty ones, turning them inside out, rubbing them on to her gums, something to make it all numb, to make the aching go away.

Searching through his clothes she puts her hand on his gun. She holds it, feels its weight, raises it up, points it at his face, holds it to her own. Caresses the trigger, pretends to squeeze.

Later, in the bathroom, grinding her jaw, staring down the mirror, she takes a pair of scissors and starts to cut at her hair.

*

Late November in the world in which he's still alive. Winter is coming, Diwali is here. The city is lit up at night, fireworks explode in the chill, wedding venues are crammed to bursting, bridegrooms on horses ride in the presence of drummers, elephants march along the highway in the mist, the markets are overflowing, their cash registers are ringing. Strings of red-and-gold tumble down the front of buildings, twinkling, gift-wrapping Delhi.

*

I called him from college and said I wanted to talk. I'd made a decision, I was tired. He told me to come over but I refused, I said I'd meet him in another place, so we agreed on a Chinese restaurant we both knew, a family place in Green Park, frayed around the edges with Formica tables and frosted-glass booths. He sounded amused on the phone. He said he'd be there in an hour. When I got there he was already waiting for me, looking half wild, puffy in the bad light, plain ugly, at once familiar and unknown to me. I sat down opposite. He went to touch my hand. I pulled it away and this caused him to laugh. He lit a cigarette and he asked what this was all about. Had I left home, was I moving in with him now? The smile on his face said he knew that wasn't the case, but I shook my head anyway and told him, No, nothing like that. I said I couldn't see him any more, that was all, it was too painful for me, too much to take, I was worn down, I couldn't trust him, I didn't know who he was any more. I had college to think about, my exams, my future. He listened to me patiently and then he told me it wasn't the case, because he was my future, and he wouldn't let me go.

I shook my head. He asked me very casually what happened to the NRI. The smile that grew around his mouth suggested he knew more than he let on. I stared at him a long time and in a whispered voice I told him to leave me alone. I got up to go to the bathroom. I left him sitting at the table, watching me.

But walking along the soiled tiled corridor at the back of the restaurant I suddenly heard someone behind following fast. It was him, he was bearing down on me with an excited look in his eyes. I hurried forward, pushed open the door and tried to make it into a cubicle to lock myself in, but he was too fast, he followed me even there, caught me before I made it through, pushed me into the cubicle with him and put one hand over my mouth to stop me crying out. Then he took his hand away, fell to his knees and removed my jeans.

I said no. But I couldn't pull myself away from it. I'm there again and he's going down on me. He's moving his tongue between my legs and I'm bracing my arms against the walls, closing my eyes and biting my lip until it bleeds.

THREE

Delhi in the winter is colder than a person from the outside can possibly imagine. There was a time when the sun would shine, but that time has gone. In its place there is the grey of pollution and the dirty clouds of freezing fog that roll into the buildings, like cotton wool wiped along the back of a filthy neck, clinging to the city in a frozen, depthless sky.

To not feel the sun, to see it only as a faint disc, like a silver tablet dissolving into water. What a terrible thing.

· · ·

The moment comes, sometime around the middle of the day, when you finally feel that the sun might come. And then it is gone again.

This would be fine if the houses were not built exclusively for the heat. If they were insulated you could retreat indoors and wait. But there's no insulation, no radiators, no carpets, and the walls that stay mercifully cool in the summer are icy now, the windows and doors let the unchecked cold seep in through their gaps, their porous borders inept against this dread. It is impossible to get warm. The cold goes into your nerves, invades your bones. It feels as if animals are gnawing at them. You sleep in silence, in blankets, fully clothed.

Despite all this happening year upon year, no one seems to have learned; everyone is surprised. In the summer, when the heat can kill, an old man goes out in a vest, shirt and sweater and cycles to and fro in the midday sun without so much as breaking a sweat. In the winter he just freezes to death.

.   .   .

Even sitting in your car you just cannot get warm. The engine blows out artificial heat, only giving a headache, inducing you to fall asleep at the wheel. As if poison is being pumped in. The word "filament" repeats in your brain.

And the men crouch in blankets, unmoving, lining the streets.

December and January, suspended animation, when the fire of north Indian blood is dimmed. Rage crawls inside itself. I crawl inside myself too. As if I've been placed inside a matchbox, in a doll's house.

*

The end, when it came, was unexpected. It was all tied up with the girl in the other tower. She never made it to Canada. She didn't even make it out of Delhi. She died right there on the day of her escape. I'd lost sight of her for a long time, I didn't think of her at all. Then I came home from college on a freezing afternoon and she was at the bottom of her tower, a crowd around her body and a pool of blood around her head.

. . .

Aunty is ablaze with the news. She shepherds me into my room. From my window we see the bedroom and a trail of sheets still coming out of it like spilt guts reaching halfway to the ground. She'd made a rope of them but had fallen almost as soon as she'd climbed out. She'd fallen, fallen all the way past the balconies with pot plants, frightening the pigeons—a short intake of air, a scream, and then silence, her brain open on the concrete.

Her father must have found out about the affair, about her boyfriend, about her plans to elope with him. Something must have happened, he must have stopped her from going, maybe he locked her up like Aunty used to say, and the window was her only escape. It made the papers, February 2001. The boyfriend, who had been waiting at the bottom of the tower with tickets and passport in hand, and who had then seen her fall, was arrested on the influence of her father. He spent two months as an undertrial in Tihar Jail.

*

That same night I drove to him in a daze. I had no one else to turn to. I told him about the girl in the window, what had happened to her, how she'd fallen trying to escape and how she'd died. I was distraught, unreasonably upset. My distress seemed to animate him. A spark was triggered in his eyes. We got drunk and smoked and held one another, talking about the shortness of lives.

The next morning I woke early, hung-over and unsure of myself. I left quietly, and on a whim went shopping. I took an auto to South Extension. Shopping to forget. To be like any other girl.

But I saw her brains on every piece of pavement I stepped on and her blood in the strands of every stranger's hair. Even so I bought a pair of jeans I liked from the Levi's store.

*

She sits with the Businessman in the club. They've cordoned off an area in the dark. There are indulgent waiters exclusively for them, segregation created through orbiting bodies of lesser wealth. The music is loud, people know who he is. She is known by association. And even those who don't know understand they must be very important. People to be reckoned with. She is seen here as a still life, painted in the chiaroscuro of carefully concealed lights that bring out a feature here and there, plunging it back into the velvet dark. In the middle of all of them she looks imperious, and with the coke in her this is how she feels. Yes, to anyone watching this girl she must look cold as moonlight, marble hard. She barely moves, just sits beside him as he talks and drinks and plots, before she goes to the bathroom for another line.

*

Waking with no memory. Fear from the belly up. Then remembering. Driving the car through red lights, speeding at dark through the fog, a brain overloaded with coke. These mornings alone are the worst. Wrapped up in a ball, trying not to remember myself.

.   .   .

But if there was anything left over in the packet I'd do it right away. And you can't live without your shades. You can't live without your blacked-out car. You can't live without your driver and gun. You can't live without the five-star rooms, without the guarded compounds. The houses of the rich are sealed compartments, and the houses of the poor are open to the world. Everything you want, anything at all. Delhi is the sound of construction, of vegetable vendors and car horns. Of crows bursting up out of the blackness and diving back down.

*

I am at his place, back from shopping for my jeans. It's about midday. For a moment I waver, think to go home, to leave him there, but instead I go inside.

He is sitting in the living room waiting for me. Immediately I know something is wrong. The look on his face has changed, the look of the previous night has gone. Right away he sneers at me, he says, Do you know what I was thinking? That it should have been you who died. At least she had the courage to leave.

I stand looking at him for a while without words, then I walk to the bedroom. But he gets up and follows me, comes into the room, snatches the shopping bag from my hands and says, So what did you buy? He dumps the jeans out on to the bed and with a look of disdain he walks out of the room. Before I know what's happening he comes back in holding a pair of scissors and he's taking the jeans and slicing into them, jerking slits all down the legs, stabbing them in a frenzy until the jeans are in shreds.

But that doesn't satisfy him, so when he's finished with the jeans he goes to the wardrobe where my things are kept, the clothes he's bought for me, my books, my keepsakes and souvenirs, and he's taking the scissors to these, flailing without reason, slicing through anything that's there, jabbing at them with such violent intent. I try to stop him, I run his way and pull him back, but he's too strong for me, he turns and throws me to the floor. When he's done cutting my things, he scoops the remains up into his arms and carries them to the balcony. I run after him in time to see him throw them over the edge. I'm screaming at him, I'm crying, shouting incoherent words, beating with my fists. He's standing there delighted with his work. Goading me, saying since I won't leave, he'll expose me, he'll show everyone what I am, what I've done, he'll send the photos to my family, he'll paste them on the college walls.

He looks at me, panting, grinning, laughing out loud, laughing at our entire world, and the scissors are in his hand. He holds the blades up in the air and brings them down to his other hand to cut into his own flesh.

I don't remember much of what happened next. I know I was trying to pull the scissors away and at the same time he was grabbing me by my wrist, spinning me around, shoving me to the ground. Then he was kicking me over and over in the stomach, the chest, in the legs, my head. Lifting me up by the throat, almost holding me in the air. I'm looking into his eyes and I can't see anyone I know. The ball of a fist closes, springs forward from the hip. There's an ocean of white spray, and a body is on the ground, and a hotness that tastes of metal blood.

. . .

Scrambling to the door, falling down the stairs, out on to the street, crawling around on my hands and knees, palming the concrete, he's kicking me as I go. This is where Ali intervenes. He turns up from nowhere, pulls him away, enough for me to stagger to my feet. And Ali is shouting out, Run, madam. Please. Run.

Fumbling for my keys, climbing inside the car, getting the engine started, driving away from him. In the rear-view mirror he's stripping off his clothes, howling at the sky, dancing naked in the road.

*

Open your eyes. Open your fucking eyes. He touches my face with his fingers. Kisses my cheek, kisses my temples, kisses my nose— Close your eyes, he says, kissing the lids.

*

She told the Businessman in the end that she had money trouble, that she needed a job. He said he could put her on the payroll, give her a salary and a position in one of his companies. She didn't have to turn up; she only had to take care of herself.

The fact of this job she relayed to Aunty and Uncle, and Aunty relayed it to everyone else, and soon everyone was placated when it came to the surface of things.

*

After he beat me the police came. Ali had run to the outpost and called them before returning to pull him away from me. When they turned up I had already gone, but he was still naked in the street, laughing, beating Ali in my place. He tried to beat them too when they came, he knocked one to the ground before they managed to overpower him. Then they beat him with their lathis until he fell unconscious.

It was Ali who also called his parents. It was his parents who used their money and influence to make the police disappear. His parents, living only a few miles away in south Delhi.

.   .   .

They committed him to a psychiatric ward the next day. He was inside that place for three months, February to April. Locked up and tied down.

*

I drove home to Aunty that afternoon and cried into her arms. I cried without restraint and she cleaned the wounds, put ice on my face, washed the blood off me, took the bloodied clothes away. The guards downstairs and some neighbours had seen me and come to the door, but Aunty curtly shooed them off. Later, when Uncle came home, she told him someone had tried to rob me near college, had tried to steal my car and I'd fought back stupidly but had escaped. Only the face had been touched, nothing more. She was at pains to point this out. A silly girl, that's what she is. A foolish girl. She told me this would happen one day. She always hated that car. But never once did she ask what really went on.

Terrified, I waited the rest of that day for him to call, for him to turn up at the door. But nothing came that day. And the next day nothing came.

.   .   .

I sat in my room. My body stopped hurting, my bruises healed. Then I went with Aunty on visits, watching the street outside, smiling politely to the other women when we arrived, answering all their questions with a nervous smile. But bracing myself every time the phone rang at night, imagining Aunty's face reacting to his voice, his words. I checked my own phone, held it in my hand as I slept. Waiting for the call. But there was no call, no knock on the door. Nothing came.

*

We live in luxury now. Unable to hold the pain of Delhi inside, it is better to orbit it from space. I sit in the back of the Businessman's car, climate controlled, inoculated, floating beyond the city in a blacked-out throne. We glide through traffic, accelerate round corners, move past red lights as if they're not there, through the charred streets of the tombs of my ancestors, the flaming oil drums and the ragged men, and all the places we have known. At night it's as if we're underwater, lights quivering in the haze of coke, glowering buses pulling across the lanes. Ghosts drift by in rickshaws, women dangle babies from the edges of motorcycles. Drowning in light and fog and noise, men stream into the road. They look into the window when the traffic stops, but no one sees me at all.

*

Inside the hospital they fed him their drugs. They tied him to a bed and injected him with many things. For days he was raging, incandescent. Saying Shiva was with him in the room.

Then he was calmed, put under their control. They began to counsel him. They challenged his beliefs. They talked to him about what he knew and what he saw. They wore him down this way, and he grew compliant. He believed what they said to him and recognized that what he believed was not the truth. Later, when they agreed to release him, it was on the condition that he renounce what he'd always thought. They made him sign a piece of paper that said Shiva did not exist.

. . .

When he came out of that place his parents took him back to his apartment. They flew his fiancée over from the States and they all stayed together for several weeks, until the end of May, and then, convinced he would be all right again, they left him in Ali's care. Ali, who promised to be with him day and night.

I retreated into my studies in those months. I blocked him from my mind as best I could, devoted myself to college instead. In May I sat my final exams, half expecting him to be there when I left the hall.

At the end of May, late at night, someone called me on my cellphone, five or six rings, enough to bring me out of sleep. But before I could think to answer, the ringing stopped. I spent the rest of the night clutching the phone tight, my eyes open in the dark.

*

The Businessman had other girlfriends. In London, in Bombay, in Delhi. But she didn't care. She had no illusions about him. And he still looked after her. He found her a small apartment in Defence Colony, a barsati near the market in B Block, a small one-bedroom flat on the roof of one of the large houses there. She moved out of Aunty's the next day. The goodbyes were brief. The coke she did in her room right then made it manageable, completely without consequence.

The barsati was bare, unfurnished. Only a bed, a table and a chair, a few rugs, naked bulbs, a couple of cups and glasses in the kitchen area. Nothing on the walls, empty shelves. The city came in from everywhere. She stood on the roof and looked out over the colony, the city. There was no one here to claim her, no one telling her what to do. She went back inside, switched off the fan and cut another line.

In this room, in silence, staring at the ceiling fan, lying completely alone, no longer waiting, she felt the bliss she'd been searching for from the start.

*

He and Ali were back in his apartment and everything went well at first. He kept regular hours, took the pills he'd been given dutifully, exercised and slept like never before. He didn't touch a drop of alcohol. His eyes took on a steady shine.

But after a few weeks things started to slip. He was restless, didn't sleep so well, and soon enough he was awake throughout the night. Ali sat with him in the living room or by the bed, exhausted, talking with him, smoking cigarettes, playing cards, but he had no luck. So they began to go out and drive again, but with Ali now in the passenger seat. They'd drive around the city, then they'd go out to the dhabas on the highway to eat.

It was here that he began to open up to Ali, to talk about the hospital and what they made him do there, what they did to him, but Ali confessed he didn't understand a word of it, it made no sense to him, he thought it was black magic and the doctors were all crazy themselves for saying Shiva didn't exist. Shiva, Allah, God, they were around us all the time, it was plain to see.

*

I know all this because I met Ali again, quite by chance. He'd found work as a driver for an associate of the Businessman, he'd clawed his way up and was sober and smartly dressed. He had a daughter now too, she was three months old. His knowledge of the city was unparalleled.

We met as I came out of a club in GK with the Businessman very late one night. There were many drivers standing waiting for us in the desolate colony street, empty besides the stray dogs and the humming lights and the expensive cars under the drivers' watchful eyes. Ali was among them—I was climbing into the back of the car when I heard his voice calling out to me. His voice brought back everything and I stopped and began to tremble, so when he came towards me the other drivers held him back as if he were mad. But I regained myself and said it was OK. We stood facing each other for a moment before I nodded at him and climbed into my car.

*

I got Ali's number from one of the other drivers and I called him the next day, asking him to come and see me when he had finished work. He arrived at my building late at night in an autorickshaw. I'd been waiting for him, unable to think of anything else, unable to go out. When I heard him I went down, handed over my car keys and told him to drive.

We drove around the city that night. He told me everything he knew.

*

Ali arrived at the apartment on the morning of June 7 to find that some bags had been packed. He told Ali he was going away, heading to the mountains the long way round, the way he loved to go, stopping off first in Jaipur, driving through Rajasthan and Punjab to Pathankot, close to the border, through the desert. From there he didn't know, maybe Ladakh or maybe Parvati, he would decide on the journey.

.   .   .

Ali expected him to leave straightaway, but for some reason he hesitated. He sat in the flat waiting in silence for something—he wouldn't say what—so that by the time he climbed into the car the sun had already set. He handed Ali a bag of money, eighty thousand rupees, and gave him the keys to the apartment, telling him to look after it while he was gone. Live in it, he said, bring your wife, be happy. He told him he'd be back in a couple of months. But Ali couldn't leave things like that. He insisted he'd drive with him some of the way.

*

When they were out of Delhi on the highway they stopped to eat at a dhaba. That's where he and Ali said goodbye. They went inside and ate chicken and dal as a last meal. In an effort to prolong the departure they had some whisky.

It was one in the morning and they were still sitting drinking as the trucks and cars and buses flew by, as the drivers drifted in and got drunk in the heavy night. They watched the lights and grew drunk too, one whisky after another, they talked about the past, argued, laughed, embraced. Ali told him his wife was expecting and that he would be a father soon and they ordered another whisky to toast this fact.

Around two, not yet completely wasted, he told Ali it was time to leave. He wanted to make Bikaner in good time, to get there by breakfast. They called over one of the old men who sat behind the counter and the three of them together found a truck that would take Ali back to the city. He paid the bill, gave Ali more money for his new baby, they embraced once more, and then he stood beside his car as he waved Ali's truck on to the road.

*

I drifted away from the Businessman in the end. Nothing spectacular. It just happened like that. I still see him around here and there, now and then. We're still on good terms. He paid for my apartment for another year, and by the time this ran out I'd found a real job for myself.

. . .

One of the last big nights I'm with him we're in a night-club, drinking champagne, it's the VVIP section, the coke is plentiful and barely concealed. We're with his rich and powerful friends.

The men, they're all at one table, the men and me, talking about business, the latest expensive watches, which airline has the finest first-class service, which politicians are favourable to use. The wives are at another table, they talk about the new Chanel store that is going to open here soon, discuss whether they will summer in a Swiss chalet this year or London again. They don't talk to me, don't like to acknowledge I exist. I don't ever sit with them. I don't care. These women are driven home early in the night. Because of the children, because of their parents, because of their reputation. Because, because, because.

Then the whisky comes out, the deals are made. This is where the real pleasure begins.

. . .

I step away from this near the end and go up to the roof to see the morning arrive. I walk out the door and slowly to the edge, high above the city, stand up on the wall and look down on the construction sites that are below. Vast construction, building the future city, the cranes and the sun all together as one. I flick my cigarette over the edge. Watch idly to see if it will hit anyone. Think briefly about stepping off myself.

All the workers' faces appear to me, caught between the pale sunrise and the artificial light, men, women, children, slaves to Laxmi, getting the job done. I think for a moment I can see his face among them.

The strangest emptiness here.

The most deafening emptiness here.

The knowledge that I don't belong.

*

But I still visited Aunty from time to time. We met on good terms, she asked my opinion on certain things. I sat in the living rooms of those chattering women to hear them talk. About this scandal and that, about servants and marriage and divorce. And they talk about 9/11 too, about the imminent Muslim threat. One woman says that Pakistan is behind it all, and another replies, At least now America will know our true worth.

And Aunty, she talks about us Hindus. She says, Us Hindus never hurt anyone in this world, we're the most peace-loving people on earth. If anything, we're too kind. We only defend ourselves when we're provoked, and we're always being provoked. But what can we do? It's our fate to be abused.

*

A year later, from sunset to rising sun, when all the dust has settled, I drop acid again in the Himalayas, where the stars are in the sky with Shiva, and Parvati is in her valley with me. Shiva and Parvati, the two of them sailing across the night in chariots big as join-the-dot stars.

From this high up in the mountains you can picture a great flood sweeping across India, from the southern ocean up through the jungles and the plains. But I'm not looking down on India tonight, only up at the constellations and the snow-capped mountains and the glaciers that are glinting in gunmetal grey with the smell of apple orchards in their wake.

In a simple concrete room built on the hillside far away, the second movement of Beethoven's Fourth Piano Concerto plays. Then the usual psytrance that marks this place. But in the orchard the noise doesn't rise above a whisper and this is where the acid holds sway.

That familiar ache, the glimmering skull. There is nothing like this valley, where Shiva dances through the mountaintops with serpents around his head, leaving trails and cosmic explosions, the whole night echoing conciliatory sounds, the constellations rippling as if a rock has been thrown into the sky. Everything has a pulse and a heart to beat here, I see them with my open eyes. Shiva and Parvati too, flitting like a pair of hummingbirds. I watch this dance for hours.

. . .

But when the first tendrils of light creep in, it's time to say goodbye. Coiling round one another, they vanish from me for ever. I wave at them as they go, poke my tongue out and skip around the orchards like a loon before collapsing on the ground.

In this new and empty world to which I belong, goats trot along chalk paths, men kindle fires on the slopes, women build them in their houses under blackened pots, smoke seeping through the roof tiles. Music meanders from temples on the morning wind, dipping in and out, suddenly louder, quieter again, and all the purple flowers of the valley are set ablaze, the sun burning up the mountainside.

The haze dissolves to a deep and lasting blue and the moon like a pelvis sinks to the Ganga's base. I put my hands in the grass, feel the earth beneath my feet, see the eagles soar above, hear the insects down below. And lying on my back just like the girl I've always been, I watch the clouds drift and glow across the roof of the world, becoming newspaper headlines that tell the story of my life, the last one saying, Fuck you, I survive.

*

I never find out about his fiancée, I never see his parents again, I never discover what happens to them, I never learn the reasons why he lied. I never know if his actions were planned or out of his hands. I let the question live with me a long time. But I'm beyond that; it makes no difference to me now. These words are his cremation, I've already watched him burn.

What's left is this: I went to the dhaba one night to see for myself, Ali told me where it was. I set off alone at 3 a.m. I drove slowly through the streets on to the highway. The silence was the kind felt at the end of a long journey, when all language has been exhausted and the mind is left alone with the things it has seen.

Around five in the morning I reached the place just as the sky was beginning to turn, pulling up alongside the trucks and the coaches and the flashing neon sign. I sat in my car for what seemed like an age, but in the end I didn't go in. I watched the entrance instead, saw the men asleep on the charpoys outside, a few still drinking at the tables within, who in the blue light of dawn looked so lonely and frail. Out in the desert where the sun should have been, the horizon was disfigured by the new cities. I drove off again.